A grim expression was settling over Sheriff Watson's
face. "Word's come in that three of Stockton's boys
went treasure hunting. Tried to find some booty left
by Kid Thomas' brother when he got sent up for
robbing the payroll."

"Who got killed?" Slocum took a wild shot at what
had happened. Only something of real importance
would roust Sheriff Watson from Durango after the
town got shot up.

"The marshal. The former marshal."

"So you're going after them?"

"Don't go sticking your nose where it don't belong,
Slocum," came Sullivan's cold voice. "This don't
concern you none!"

OTHER BOOKS BY JAKE LOGAN

JAKE LOGAN

VIGILANTE JUSTICE

BERKLEY BOOKS, NEW YORK

VIGILANTE JUSTICE

A Berkley Book/published by arrangement with
the author

PRINTING HISTORY
Berkley edition/October 1985

ISBN: 0-425-08279-2

A BERKLEY BOOK ® TM 757,375
Berkley Books are published by The Berkley Publishing Group,
200 Madison Avenue, New York, NY 10016.
The name "BERKLEY" and the stylized "B" with design are trademarks
belonging to Berkley Publishing Corporation.
PRINTED IN THE UNITED STATES OF AMERICA

1

New Mexico Territory had been unusually dry through the winter and now, as John Slocum rode north along the Rio Puerco, he saw evidence of a dry spring. Occasional April winds kicked up and forced him to lower his head to keep his watering eyes free of dust, but mostly he held his head up and enjoyed the solitude and majestic beauty of the Jemez Mountains.

"Days like this," he told his dappled gray mare, "that it makes me think of settlin' down and doing some ranching. Sunshine, good grazing if it ever decides to rain, nobody jostling your elbow."

Slocum fell into silence as the mare picked her way through a tumble of fist-sized rocks along the bottom of a dry mountain arroyo. This deep river bed ought to have been running bank to bank with crystal clear runoff from the higher slopes. The sparse winter of '80–'81 snowpack robbed this particular arroyo of its liquid treasure. Only a few hardy creosote bushes dared turn gray-green, but Slocum knew that true spring had come because of the swollen buds on the mesquites' thorny limbs. The deep-rooted tree never blossomed until the last of the cold weather had gone.

Slocum rode along lost in thought, letting the sure-footed horse pick her way up the far slope and go even deeper into the mountains. He had no particular destination in mind after leaving Albuquerque almost a week earlier. Santa Fe had been a thought, but only a passing one. The Santa Fe Ring's politics didn't set well with him and only boded trouble for the footloose, even if he was an ex-Confederate officer in a land run by other ex-Confederates. He had headed to the west, then up in the general direction of Farmington, thinking to work his way to Durango, through Ute country, and on up to Denver.

Denver had honest work for the likes of him, Slocum knew. The thriving towns always did. Around dry New Mexico he wasn't likely to find much work as a ranch hand. The herds here would be smaller and the ranchers less likely to hire new men. And from what he'd heard, it wasn't too safe working for any of the farmers. The cattlemen didn't take kindly to their presence—and it was getting worse.

Besides, Slocum wanted to stay a few days at the Planter's House. The Overland Stage might still use it as an office and way-station. If it did, Slocum looked to pick up a few double eagles off passengers who thought they knew poker odds better than he did.

He scratched at the bugs chewing away at his hide. He needed more than a few suckers in a game of poker. He needed a good, long bath. Slocum urged his mare up another steep slope and then onto a more level space. With any luck, they might be able to make Durango in the next day or two.

"It's oats for you then, old girl," he told the horse, patting her on the neck. "And for me, a bath and some whiskey." The mere thought of that amber liquid burning its way down his gullet warmed Slocum enough to keep him going. The days of travel stretched endlessly in front of him—and behind.

He preferred to think of the present only. The past held too many bad memories.

A gunshot echoing down a side canyon brought the memories of the War years back—the War and a dozen other scrapes he'd been in with men shooting at him. The whine of a ricochet came later, much later. It was then that Slocum actually reached for the ebony-handled Colt Navy he carried in a cross-draw holster.

More gunfire. He relaxed a mite when he decided the gunshots came from some distance off. The canyons, mountain peaks, and clear, crisp spring air made the sound seem closer than it really was.

"Let's keep on in this direction," he muttered, more to himself than to the horse. But the gray mare understood both sentiment and the danger of being caught up in a fight. Slocum hadn't gone through Santa Fe because of the unrest there. He had thought he would avoid all the politics and assassinations going on by coming this way. And maybe he would. The shots might be a hunter.

They still sounded like lighter-caliber handguns to him, though. Nobody hunted these mountains with only a handgun. Nobody but a fool. A Sharps .69-caliber was barely big enough to bring down some of the grizzlies in these parts. Even the deer didn't take kindly to careless hunting. Slocum had seen more than one hunter killed by a buck in rut. The velvet might still be on the bucks' racks right now, but he didn't want to consider anyone damn fool stupid enough to give the deer a chance to scrape it off on belly or arm or leg bone.

Another gunshot. Closer.

Handguns. The only thing that's being hunted is a man, he thought. He spurred his horse to a trot. Reaching the end of the canyon might provide him with a chance to avoid even seeing another human being before he got to Durango and that hot bath.

The clatter of the shod hooves sounded like continuously rolling thunder to Slocum. He hoped those in the side canyon were too wrapped up in their gunplay to notice this new sound. The idea of finding a place to hole up appealed to him more and more. Let whoever was kicking up such a fuss pass on by. Slocum started to take more care, having the mare walk gingerly on solid rock, go downslope and then back up to confuse the trail. Every time he could find gravel instead of sand in an arroyo bottom, he chose that path. The horse snorted her dislike for the hard surfaces but gamely continued, as if realizing that only trouble lay behind.

"Now that's a fine sight," Slocum said as they emerged from the long, rocky canyon. A grassy valley stretched between mountain peaks. While sparse from the drought, the grass provided a welcome meal for his horse. Slocum dismounted and stretched out under a tree, hat tipped over his eyes to shield them from the sun. A little rest couldn't hurt; he had left those noisy sons of bitches back in the mazes of mountain canyons. Rest and then be on his way, he figured.

Slocum drifted off into a light sleep, only to come fully awake, pistol in hand, when he heard the sounds of horses. He shot to his feet and soothed his horse to keep her from neighing.

"Might not mean anything," he said softly. But Slocum didn't believe that for an instant.

The light breezes quieted and snippets of conversation

drifted to where Slocum waited impatiently. He didn't like the parts he heard, not one bit.

"... around here someplace. Those are his tracks. I know it. Son of a..."

"Time to go," Slocum said, swinging back into the saddle. The gray protested and tried to balk, but Slocum gently insisted. His years spent as a hunter had given him great insight into how the hunted felt—and this was the feeling building up inside him. He hadn't done anything, but those men had to be a posse. They hunted somebody down. Slocum had seen enough posses to know they usually didn't much care who they caught. One warm body was as good as another to string up. Posses cared less for justice than they did for the relief they got seeing some poor bastard's heels kicking in the wind, a rope around his neck. They could ride on home and brag about how they'd saved everybody or how revenge had been exacted from the guilty party.

If they found they'd made a mistake, then that only gave them the excuse for another necktie party.

Slocum didn't hanker to be anybody's mistake.

He made a quick decision not to continue on his course across the open valley with its pleasant stands of cypress and juniper and pine. He turned back toward the rocky canyons he'd just left. If they thought he or whoever they chased was hell-bent for getting away, doubling back on the trail might throw them off and let him get away scot free.

"... crossed over there," came the voice during an unnatural lull in the wind.

Slocum urged his horse to greater speed. On the softer ground the clatter of hooves against the occasional rock couldn't be heard as easily. He decided speed counted for more than complete stealth.

Slocum rode into the canyon mouth only to find a small band of men trailing the larger posse.

They didn't even bother calling out to him. One raised a carbine and loosed a round that whizzed less than a foot from Slocum's left ear. He jerked involuntarily and bent forward over the mare's neck. Slocum didn't have to spur the horse. She broke into a gallop that quickly lathered her flanks.

Another bullet sought his flesh, missing by more than a yard and ricocheting off a large limestone outcropping. Dust and small rock shards rained down on Slocum as he jerked savagely on the reins and pulled the horse to shelter.

Can't outrun them. Maybe I can talk to them. Slocum quickly sized up his position. Not too bad. He had high ground, even if there wasn't much way of continuing on up the slope without being seen. Escape to either the left or right was a possibility.

Settling the matter looked to be easier and safer. Those owlhoots fired sporadically now at anything moving. With the spring breezes combing through undergrowth and trees, just about everything moved.

"Hello down there!" Slocum shouted. "Hold your fire!"

"Son of a bitch's giving up," came a disappointed voice.

"My name's Slocum. Why're you shooting at me? I just rode into this part of the country."

"Not only a backshooter, but a damn liar as well," grumbled an unseen vigilante.

"Haven't shot anyone," Slocum called, a sinking feeling in his guts. They wanted blood, not reason. "Rode into Albuquerque from Tucson about three weeks ago. Came up along the Rio Puerco, heading for Durango and intending to go on to Denver."

Slocum's quick reflexes saved him. He heard the scuffle of worn boot leather on sandstone. He whipped around, the .31 Colt coming into aim perfectly. He got off three quick shots before the vigilante could even raise his rifle. The man screeched like a scalded pig and vanished from sight. Slocum doubted he'd even touched the man.

"Don't want to shoot you," he called out. "Don't even know why you're coming after me like this."

"Shut your lyin' mouth, Stockton. We're gonna string you up for all you done!"

"I'm not this Stockton fellow," Slocum called. "Never even heard of him." The sounds from below told him they were ready to launch an all-out frontal attack, his gunfire be damned. Whoever this Stockton was, they wanted him bad.

Slocum reholstered his pistol and drew forth his Winchester. If he was going to have to do some serious shooting, he wanted the proper tool for the task. Slocum settled down, old feelings rising within him. It had been like this before. Too many times before.

During the War, he had been more than a sniper. He had been one of the best. He scouted, found a good spot looking over the field of battle, set up his bivouac, and looked for the flash of a Union officer's gold braid in the sun. Without their officers, the Yankees had a harder time keeping order in the field.

With his Spenser carbine, he had created massive disorder in Union ranks.

The sighting, the exhalation, the slow, even pull on the trigger, followed by the hard buck of the rifle against his shoulder, all came to him now. From below, one injured vigilante screamed out in pain. Not a clean shot, but Slocum didn't much care. He just wanted them to give up and let him be.

They came on, shouting what they'd do to any Stockton they caught.

Four more rounds convinced them that none of them might reach Slocum before he got them in his sights. He'd

fired five times and found a fleshy target with three of the
Winchester's bullets. The vigilantes fell back to regroup.

". . . an army up there, Marsh!" complained one of those
below.

"There's only the one. Must be Ike hisself."

Slocum took the time to reload both his rifle and his Colt.
He started thinking of escape, since talking wasn't getting
him anywhere. He had no desire to slaughter the men below,
and he'd be damned if he was going to let them shoot him
up any.

Slocum rose quietly and took the horse's reins. The dusty
ledge ran back toward the canyon floor. He took it, using
the granite and limestone boulders for what cover he could.
Slocum thought he was going to get away from the posse
when one of them cried out, "He ain't up there. He's headin'
back into the canyon!"

Slocum climbed into the saddle. His horse had rested for
a spell and this allowed the mare to give him the speed he
wanted. Although the trail was narrow and rocky, the mare
managed to keep her footing until they came to a cross
canyon. Slocum turned into it, glad for the sandy-bottomed
arroyo. The horse galloped along, but Slocum heard the
sounds of pursuit from behind.

He had no idea where this canyon headed. He might be
riding into a box canyon and a trap for all he knew. He
might get a ways ahead, dismount, and pick off the vigilantes as they rode past. It wasn't anything new to him,
after all. But the idea of killing that many men didn't set
well. Better to keep on and hope his luck turned for the
better.

It didn't. He stopped the instant he recognized the for-
mation of a box canyon in front of him, but by then it was
too late to turn around. He heard joyous whoops and hollers
from the posse.

Disgusted with his bad luck and tired of being chased for something he didn't do—whoever this Ike Stockton was, he had a powerful lot of enemies—Slocum readied himself. Resting prone on a large boulder, he squinted into the mouth of the canyon, waiting.

He knocked the third rider off his horse. Then he worked forward, winging both the second and lead men. This kept the other three back far enough to keep them from opening fire on him. By the time they figured out where he had been to make the shots, Slocum had moved on to another position.

He scowled at what he saw. He had wounded only four of the six men. Two of the ones he'd just knocked out of the saddle he had already hit when he made his first attempt to speak to the posse. Not a one dead, maybe none of them even at the point of wanting to stop fighting.

Slocum concentrated, looking for the killing shot now. Nothing less would get him out of the canyon alive.

The fusillade of angry bullets forced him back to cover. He didn't worry unduly. Let them waste their ammunition. But what did worry him was their tenacity. They must really hate this Stockton, to keep coming on so strong.

"I'm not Stockton!" he shouted. Echoes rumbled down the canyon, distorting his words, turning the tones into another man's. "My name's John Slocum."

His answer came in a hail of bullets. One fragment bouncing off a rock grazed his cheek and left behind a bloody smear. More angry than hurt, Slocum crawled around to find a better position.

Another torrential outpouring of bullets killed his horse. He jerked around and watched the valiant animal keel over, kicking her heels only once. Then she lay still in the warm afternoon sun.

Burning with cold fire, Slocum slithered to the side of a boulder and peered around. Three men came at him. He started firing. He missed all three, but the sounds of their fright fed his grim intention of seeing them all as dead as the mare.

Slocum waited, knowing that the posse would come back looking for him if he didn't fire. Curious, cautious, they'd come. And then they'd die.

He frowned when he heard the sharp reports of at least a dozen rifles. The bullets never found a rock to smash against this deep in the canyon. It was almost as if . . . Slocum dared to hope.

He got to the top of a rock and looked down the canyon in time to see his would-be killers getting into their saddles and riding like the gates of hell had been opened behind them.

Coming up the crossing canyon, back from the grassy valley, rode the first band of vigilantes Slocum had encountered. They fired volley after volley at the retreating men.

Slocum puzzled over this. He had thought the two groups were fragments of a larger posse. Obviously, he'd been wrong. This band ran off the ones who'd been so intent on gunning him down. Slocum watched as a few of the new band chased after the others. A half-dozen sighted him and started up toward him. He waved. If they'd saved him from the posse that had mistaken him for this Ike Stockton, Slocum figured they couldn't be out for his blood.

"Hello!" he shouted. "Thanks for getting them off my ass."

The man in the lead waved to him. Slocum began to relax. Seeing that it would be a few minutes before they'd reach him, he slid off the rock and walked back up the draw to where the mare now attracted the mountain scavengers. Brown beetles nipped at the dead flesh and flies in a cloud thick enough to turn the air blue and black buzzed all around.

Slocum unfastened the cinches and pulled his saddle free. Then he took off the bridle and bit.

"You deserved better. You deserved oats and a nice stable," he said to the horse. He turned away. The horse's eyes had remained open and stared accusingly at him, as if this were all his fault.

Three of the men who'd rescued him from the posse rode up. They didn't dismount. The one Slocum took to be the leader quickly sized up all that had happened.

"They got your horse, eh?" he said.

Slocum had nothing to say to the obvious. What put him on his guard was the man's tone. He wasn't any friendlier than the other posse had been.

Without trying to appear obvious about it, Slocum put down his gear and rested his rifle across the saddle where he could get to it in a hurry. He slid his left hand along his gunbelt until his thumb lifted off the leather thong over the Colt's hammer. He didn't reach for the pistol. Yet.

"They thought I was somebody named Stockton. You know him?"

"Think they're gettin' cleverer, Jeb?" one of the other riders asked his leader. "A spy amongst us would let them find out every little thing we're doin'."

"I'm no spy," Slocum said, a coldness settling inside him again. "I'm on my way to Denver. Going up through Durango. Came from Tucson."

"You believe him, Doc? You, Bent?" Both men shook their heads. The leader, Jeb, rested both hands on the pommel and leaned forward, weight on his stirrups. "Can't say I much believe you, either."

Slocum tensed, ready to go for his pistol.

"Don't go tryin' that, mister," said Jeb. The man tipped his head to one side and let his eyes dart upslope before coming to rest coldly on Slocum.

Slocum saw the glint of sunlight off rifle barrels. Four, maybe five. He slowly twisted and looked in the other direction. Two more men with rifles.

"You so much as sneeze, they're gonna cut you down." Jeb seemed to take only small satisfaction in this.

"You one of Stockton's men?" Slocum asked.

"Don't matter if I am or not. What matters is if *you* are. I think you are."

The man rode slowly toward Slocum. Quicker than a snake, the man's boot slipped from the stirrup and crashed into the side of Slocum's head, sending him tumbling to the ground. Dazed, he tried to lift himself onto hands and knees.

Slocum found himself pulled erect by three of the men. Colt gone, separated from his rifle, he had nothing to defend himself with except his fists. He used them.

They knocked him to the ground again. This time, when they got him to his feet, they crudely tied his hands behind his back. He started to protest but strong hands shoved him forward, almost pushing him to the ground. Slocum realized what he might expect from these men if he got them really riled.

"I don't know what's going on, but I don't know any Stockton. I don't know who those others were and I sure as hell don't know who you are."

"Them bushwhackers?" Jeb said with venom dripping from his words. "They was part of a special militia unit Governor Wallace set up to find Stockton."

"Then you're working for this Stockton?" Slocum couldn't keep it all straight. His head rang from the blow he'd taken and fear began rising like a tide inside him when one man dismounted and the others boosted Slocum into the saddle.

Slocum turned and saw another man putting the finishing touches on the thirteen spiralling turns of a noose. It rose into the spring afternoon air, momentarily outlined itself against the blue New Mexico sky, then fell to the other side of the cottonwood limb, swinging slowly to and fro.

"We've got no love for the governor's militia. We came down from Farmington huntin' for Stockton on our own. You ain't him, but you'll do. You got to be one of his men."

"Another vigilante posse?" Slocum asked, confused.

"There's a whole raft of us runnin' around these parts. None of us much likes the other. Don't matter. We're all huntin' Ike Stockton and his men. You look to be one of them." Jeb spat, fumbled in his shirt pocket for another plug of tobacco, bit it off, and for the first time smiled.

"Boys," said Jeb, "string the son of a bitch up!"

Slocum tried to get the horse to bolt and run, but the men on the ground held onto the reins too securely. He swallowed hard when they positioned the horse under the tree limb and fitted the coarse hemp noose around his neck.

"Goodbye, backshooter. You're gonna see Ike Stockton in hell real soon."

Slocum closed his eyes and waited for the drop that would break his neck.

2

Slocum had been close to death before. That didn't make accepting it now any easier. The rope cut into the flesh of his throat and prevented him from swallowing. A rough, parched tongue came out to lick his equally dry lips. He held back a need to cry out. Worst of all, he had the urge to sneeze. The cottonwood fleece filled his nose and tickled until he could barely stand it.

But Slocum realized he wouldn't have long to endure such mild torture if Jeb and the others had their way.

In a voice calmer than he expected, Slocum said, "I'm not the one you want. I don't know anything about this. You wouldn't hang an innocent man, would you?"

Jeb rode over and peered at Slocum. The man spat, then wiped his lips and shook his head. "Don't reckon we're hangin' an *innocent* man. You don't have the look of a lamb about you, now do you?"

Something in the way the man spoke told Slocum he

might have a chance. A thin one, but still a chance. He had never been lucky at drawing to inside straights, but now he had to risk it. The only option to playing was death.

"Can't say I'm innocent. No man who goes through the War is innocent."

This drew Jeb's attention. "What outfit were you with?"

Slocum had no hesitation in answering. The horse danced about nervously below him and tightened the rope. He had to swallow twice before he got enough slack to speak. He hoped the horse wasn't too skittish. A rabbit or chicken hawk swooping down might send the animal running and leave him dangling with his heels three feet above the ground.

"Started with Jackson's Brigade. Was with him at Manassas. Through the Valley Campaign."

"The Shenandoah," mused Jeb. "Right purty, it was."

"Back to Manassas again. Beat the Yanks there again. At Gettysburg."

"What'd you do there?"

"Sharpshooter. Laid down fire to protect Pickett from Little Round Top." Even with a noose around his neck, Slocum couldn't keep the anger from his voice over that damn fool General Pickett. Slocum's brother Robert had died at Gettysburg. He still remembered the wounded crying out for water—or for the release from pain offered by a quick, merciful death.

Robert had died quick. For that Slocum had always been thankful. He twisted sideways, gasping for air. His brother's watch still rode in his vest pocket.

"Didn't much care for Pickett, did you?"

"Still don't. Will I be going to my grave cursing him for being such a fool?"

"Reckon you will," said Jeb, "but maybe not today. What was it you said brought you to these parts?"

Slocum almost sagged at this. He'd won.

"Hard discussing anything with a rope around my neck."

In a few seconds, Jeb had taken the noose off, but he didn't offer to undo Slocum's hands. They remained tied tightly behind his back.

"I was at Gettysburg," said Jeb. "Sorriest day of my life. Lost two brothers there."

Slocum began talking of the War, sounding out Jeb. He finished with, "Been drifting through this part of the country. On my way up to Denver, as I said. Wanted to avoid Santa Fe because I don't rightly like what's been going on there." Slocum knew he rode over treacherous ground with politics. He might be talking to Governor Lew Wallace's right hand man—or, worse, a man who believed the Santa Fe Ring could do no wrong.

"Bunch of horse thieves," muttered Jeb. "They'd steal a man's last nickel if they could. What they're doing to gain control of the Maxwell Land Grant and Railway Company is downright criminal, but who's to call them out on it?"

Slocum said nothing. The Maxwell Land Grant and Railway Company sounded familiar to him, but not so much that he dared comment.

"You have the look of a gunman," said Jeb.

"I was a sharpshooter during the War. Told you that."

"That Colt Navy looks well used."

Slocum had no answer for that. It had been well used, and mostly on men who got too nosy for their own good.

"Heard tell Ike Stockton's bringing in gunmen like Clay Allison. Not much happening for their kind since the Lincoln County War's over and done with."

"Heard about that. Don't know Allison. Don't know Stockton. Never heard the name before today." Slocum looked Jeb square in the eye.

Slocum's heart almost exploded in his chest when Jeb pulled out a long hunting knife and leaned forward. Slocum didn't know if the man intended to cut his ropes or his throat.

The ropes parted from a single slash of that sharp knife.

"No man's a good enough liar to make all that up on the spur of the moment. Even when his life's ridin' on it," Jeb said. "Can't say I'm sorry about doing this to you. These aren't the best of times for a stranger to be travellin' through San Juan County."

Slocum rubbed his wrists until the circulation returned. "Thanks for the warning. All I want is to be out of here as quick as I can."

Slocum heard the others grumbling. They'd wanted to see someone strung up. It didn't matter to them if their victim had anything to do with Ike Stockton or the Maxwell Land Grant and Railway Company or the Santa Fe Ring. They just wanted some blood.

Even though he didn't know the details, Slocum guessed a range war was in progress. He couldn't much blame these men for their attitudes, even if he didn't like being on the receiving end of their tender mercies. Range wars were about the nastiest form of fighting there could be. Neighbor against neighbor, sometimes brother against brother, father against son. The best Slocum could figure, the first posse that had boxed him in were ununiformed militia sent out by Governor Wallace, and generally despised by everyone locally. This group came out of Farmington and hunted down Ike Stockton, for whatever crimes he'd committed. They were one side of a war that might rage for a good long time.

Slocum intended to be two hundred miles north in Denver by the time San Juan County actually got down to open warfare.

"Ride with us back to Farmington," said Jeb. His tone indicated this wasn't a friendly request. Not wanting a bullet in the back or to be strung up on another tree limb, Slocum nodded his agreement. "Keep on that horse. Benny can ride double with somebody else."

Slocum knew this wasn't charity on their part. With him riding alone, he made an easier target if Jeb had guessed wrong about his intentions. It suited Slocum just fine, though.

"Much obliged. About all I want to do now is get a hot bath and be on my way."

He threw his gear over the horse's hindquarters and re-mounted. While Jeb let him keep both his Winchester and his Colt, Slocum knew all eyes followed him like a hunting hawk watching its earthbound prey. One mistake and he would end up a pound heavier from all the lead in his body.

Jeb rode hard, trying to catch up with the governor's militia, but the smaller band eluded them. Slocum noted the occasional splotches of red. He had done more than wing a couple of the men. He said nothing to Jeb about it, though. Slocum figured anything he said now only endangered the man's good nature.

"Let's get on back to Farmington," Jeb finally declared. "We're not going to find Ike out here today."

Six hours of hard riding brought them to the edge of the small New Mexico town. Slocum leaned forward in the saddle, bone-tired from all that had happened to him that day. The few lights burning in the town told Slocum that this wasn't an ordinary town. Those lights were grouped strangely. For a few seconds he didn't know what that meant.

Then it came to him. The same patterns were common around campsites during the War. Lanterns to light up approaches, sentries behind them, watching, waiting, rifles ready. No stray illumination to betray those in the camp.

"Stockton's got us all a bit spooked," said Jeb, noting Slocum's surprise at the way Farmington was arrayed. "Come on down. We'll get you fixed up with a meal, that bath you're hankerin' for, and a way out of town."

The last carried special emphasis in the man's words. Jeb summed up the entire town's desire to see the last of John Slocum. For Slocum's part, that suited him just fine.

No one greeted them as they rode into town. The few dour men standing around all carried rifles or shotguns. Slocum saw no trace of women or children. He might have been visiting one of Stonewall Jackson's encampments at Manassas. What little trade went on in Farmington seemed subdued, almost furtive, as if they didn't want outsiders seeing it.

"Looks like you're ready for a siege," Slocum said.

"Stockton's been coming and going a lot recently. We're gonna string that son of a bitch up one of these days."

Slocum started to ask what the man had done, then stopped. It was no concern of his if everyone in Farmington wanted Stockton's neck stretched. What mattered was that the good citizens didn't also do it to John Slocum.

"Here," Jeb said. "Get down here. We'll get a bite to eat; then you can be on your way."

Slocum started to protest. They'd been riding hard all day long and he felt a weariness that went all the way to his soul. But Jeb had saved him once that day and he might be trying to do it again. Looking around, Slocum saw no hint of friendliness anywhere. The people of Farmington, New Mexico, were as likely to shoot him in the back as talk to him.

"Be needing a horse. Mine got killed."

"I remember," Jeb said. "The stable's at the end of the main street, just off Railroad Avenue. I warn you, though, price's gonna be mighty steep. The Utes been stealing horses something fierce this winter."

"What's a fair price?"

"Well," Jeb said, rubbing his stubbly chin, "an unbroke horse might run fifty dollars. A saddle-broke one could be twice that."

Slocum stopped and stared. A hundred dollars for a horse was outrageous. But not as outrageous as going on into Colorado on foot. Getting to Durango only a handful of miles up the road would be hard without a horse. Slocum had noted how they'd spent most of the day climbing hills. The elevation had changed drastically and between Farmington and Durango it went up even more steeply.

"Might be able to buy the back legs of a saddle horse," Slocum allowed. "Too much to feed the front end if it costs a hundred dollars."

Jeb laughed and slapped Slocum on the back. "You're all right, Slocum. Come on in. Let my missus fix you something to eat."

Slocum ate in silence. The food wasn't anything fancy, but Slocum didn't mind. And the peach cobbler slid down his throat and settled in his belly in a satisfying way. He wiped his mouth and leaned back.

"Best I've had in a long time. Thank you, ma'am," he said.

The woman only nodded and left hurriedly.

"Don't blame her for the way she treats you, Slocum," said Jeb, a worried look on his face. "Stockton's brother Port came through and shot up the town and . . . well . . . he did things to some of the women." Jeb's voice turned icy. "Glad that Port's dead. Him and the other two."

"What happened?"

"Port Stockton got himself shot up. They brought his body into town for burying. We didn't want no part of him in our cemetery. Ike and eight others came in to see that Port got a good burial." Jeb heaved a deep breath. "By the time they rode out, they'd shot up the town. We killed William Baker and hit Tom Nance in the leg. That was back on March twelfth. Since then, Stockton's been snipin' and rustlin' and making life miserable around Farmington. But we'll stop him, by damn we will!"

"You bury Stockton's brother in your cemetery?"

"Stockton took him. To his spread up at Animas City, probably. Don't rightly care spit what he did with the rapin' son of a bitch. I curse the day the Stocktons came here from Texas."

"Best find that livery you mentioned and be on my way."

Slocum rose. Jeb stopped him, hand on his shoulder. "Look, Slocum, about today. Things aren't good around here. You understand?"

"Reckon I'd be doing the same in your place," Slocum lied. He turned and left Jeb and his wife and headed down to find the stables.

As he walked along Railroad Avenue, Slocum felt a dozen pairs of eyes tracking him. He kept his spine straight and his shoulders pulled back, showing no hint of fear. There was no way of telling how many itchy fingers rested on hair triggers, just begging for a reason to gun him down. Slocum vented a gusty sigh of relief when he saw the livery.

The dickering over the price of a horse went much as Jeb had warned. The owner started at a hundred dollars for a saddle-broke horse. Slocum found one decrepit old mare, too swayback for much riding, that the man would let go for sixty.

"Eats too damn much," the stable owner complained. "Can't get a good day's work from her and she don't ride worth shit, either."

"She's still got a few miles in her," Slocum said. While the horse wasn't anything near as good as the gray mare lying out in the New Mexico wilderness had been, this one was alive. Barely. Her hooves were chipped and one shoe threatened to come off. Slocum pointed this out and got the price of fixing it thrown in to the sixty dollars.

"As long as she gets me to Durango," he said.

The stable owner stiffened, and Slocum realized he had said something wrong.

"That's Stockton territory."

"Couldn't care less about that," Slocum said earnestly. "Just passing through. On my way north." He started to repeat how he was looking for work in Denver and discarded the notion. "Going on up to Wyoming. Maybe farther than that. Haven't decided."

All Slocum wanted was to be away from San Juan County and the hatred boiling like bad coffee over a campfire.

"Good luck," the stable owner said insincerely. "A lot of trouble between here and Durango."

Slocum didn't have to be told that. Ike Stockton, Ute raiding parties, Governor Wallace's militia, vigilantes— Slocum didn't find himself looking forward to the next few days at all.

He paid, saddled, and, aching in every joint, mounted and started north and east for Durango.

3

The countryside turned rockier, the mountains higher and more rugged, some of the loftier peaks retaining thick white snowpacks no matter the season. A chilly wind blew into Slocum's face, but he felt even colder thinking of the range war brewing all around him. The people in Farmington lived in an armed camp. Whatever Ike Stockton and his dead brother Port had been up to, it had everybody spooked good.

Slocum knew he was well rid of it all.

The trail wound around the sides of sheer mountains, then into a small valley leading toward Durango, Colorado. Depending on how it looked higher up, Slocum figured to go farther north through Silverton and Ouray and cross over at Poncha Pass. If the snows still hadn't begun melting, he'd cut due east from Durango to Pagosa Springs and go through Wolf Creek Pass and then on up to Denver.

About all he knew for sure was two things. He wanted away from the San Juan area and all its trouble. The other posed an even more immediate problem. The decrepit horse he rode wheezed and gasped with every step, and the sway in her back seemed to grow with every passing mile until Slocum's boot soles almost dragged the ground.

He got to alternately feeling sorry for her and wishing he could put her out of her misery with a single shot.

"Durango and we sell you," he promised. "Maybe somebody'll have use for you. There's no way you could get me to Wyoming or even to Denver." He gusted a heavy sigh and watched the white clouds of his breath halo his head. Even though it was springtime in the Rockies, the air stayed cold. It would be another month before temperatures warmed enough to make riding without a heavy coat possible.

Slocum rode through most of the day and stopped to camp early. He had been on the trail since after sundown the night before and had tired to the point of exhaustion. The horse was in little better shape. Slocum found a grassy spot where soft green shoots came up through the rocky soil and let the old nag graze. He set up camp, fixing a small campfire. The coffee he brewed tasted terrible—and it was about the sweetest thing he'd ever let slide down his gullet.

Slocum had been through hell recently. Nothing suited him better than lounging back, hot coffee in hand, looking at the sun setting over the western peaks and just enjoying the brilliant sky lit with oranges and bright whites that turned to grays and finally faded to blackness. By this time, the crystalline shards of stars came into view, virtually untwinkling through the clean, crisp, cold air.

Slocum pulled his blanket around his shoulders and rolled to one side, dozing. He came wide awake, Colt in hand, when a gunshot rang through the stillness. For long minutes, Slocum couldn't decide from which direction the shot had come. A second shot convinced him that the sounds originated from ahead on the trail.

"Damn," he muttered. "Can't get away from their posses for love nor money." Without even realizing it, his hand went to his neck and rubbed the bruised flesh where the Farmington posse's noose had abraded. The physical damage was light; the memory would linger for a good many years.

Slocum kicked dirt on the smouldering fire, making sure even the dullest ember had vanished from sight. He considered mounting and riding blindly into the night, then discarded the idea. Getting lost in the Rockies meant death, even when spring hesitantly touched the slopes. He'd heard of men wandering for days or even weeks, lost in the confusing turns and bends of canyons and parallel valleys. Right now he knew the general location of Durango and how long it would take to get there. The trail he followed was well enough blazed for him to be able to follow it even in the dark, but to do so meant riding straight into the gunfire.

Slocum thought of a dozen things he'd rather do than to continue on.

"Damn," he swore again. Slocum considered doing nothing, going back to sleep, and waiting for the trouble to blow by him. The vigilantes or whoever these folks might be couldn't be hunting him down. Any pursuit would come from behind, from the direction of Farmington.

Staying meant a chance for his own safety. Going on could get him another noose around the neck.

It might also mean someone else passing through, as he was trying to do, might end up lynched.

"Can't hurt just to take a look," he said to the horse, patting her on the neck. "We won't get involved. Just making sure we don't get into more trouble before we know it."

He saddled the horse and climbed up. The stars mocked him, telling him what a fool he was. He couldn't argue.

This was suicidal, riding out in the middle of the night with no clear idea who or what lay ahead. He rode along the well-defined trail slowly, cautiously, not wanting to make his presence known.

More gunshots came from ahead. This time Slocum heard men swearing. A shotgun blast answered the lighter pistol fire. He rode for another hundred yards, then dismounted, carefully noting where he tethered his horse. He didn't want to need a quick escape only to be unable to find the animal. As old and feeble as she was, the swayback horse provided better speed than he could make on foot.

Slocum walked three hundred yards, then dropped to his belly and snaked along the cold ground until he came to a small rise looking into a draw. A long orange tongue of flame leaped from the muzzle of a shotgun not ten feet away.

"Take that, you miserable bushwhackers! I'll see you all in hell before I pay you a goddamn cent!"

The second barrel cut loose its load. Slocum heard the heavy lead pellets whining off a rock, but no indication the man below him had hit anyone.

Slocum ducked for cover when the unseen men who were being shot at returned fire.

"Pay the toll, Billy. Ain't that much. Not worth getting your balls shot off for."

"I don't have the money. Even if I did, you wouldn't get it!" The shotgun blasted forth its deadly load again. Slocum frowned. The man below him sounded frightened, but something more than that. His voice cracked. Slocum edged forward for a better look and finally saw the man pinned down.

He was a boy, hardly older than fifteen or sixteen. The expression on his face told of his terror, but Slocum also saw the set of the body, the determination not to give in, even if it meant death.

"Can't seem to learn," he muttered to himself. He pulled out his Colt and slipped over the top of the rise, tumbling down to land beside the boy in a shower of stones and loose dirt.

"Wha—?" the boy cried, spinning around.

Slocum grabbed the shotgun and shoved it up and away. He yelped as he burned himself on the hot wound Damascus barrel.

"Cool down," Slocum ordered. "I don't know what this is all about, but I heard enough. You needing help?"

"You're not with Ike's men?" the boy asked. His deep voice had given way to adolescent shrillness again.

"Those are Stockton's men?" Slocum said, inwardly groaning. Every bit of devilment in the entire area laid itself right on Ike Stockton's doorstep.

"Who else?"

"Yeah, who else?" Slocum said. "I'm just passing through; I don't have any stake in all this. I just don't like to see people bushwhacked. That's the only reason I'm helping."

Even as he spoke, Slocum knew he lied, at least in part. Stockton had caused him a world of trouble simply by existing. This was about the only way Slocum had of getting back at the man he'd never met. It was a foolish, maybe futile, gesture, but Slocum felt the better for making it. He kept telling himself that the boy would end up buzzard meat if he didn't help.

That didn't change things much.

"They're killers," the boy said, his voice turning deeper again. "They been charging tolls on the road between Farmington and Durango for damn near a month now. I don't have the money. Even if I did, I wouldn't pay it. Not to the likes of them!"

"How many are out there?" Slocum asked, not caring about such local details.

"Not more'n five. Probably four. I don't reckon I hit any

of them. Didn't even see them."

"How many shells you got left for that?" Slocum pointed to the battered shotgun.

The boy silently held out his hand. Four shells.

"Make them count. As long as they don't know you got company, they might get careless. You know them by name?"

"Don't think so. Heard rumors Clay Allison had joined up with Ike."

"You know Allison?"

"No."

"Stay here. Shoot if you see something moving and you're sure it isn't me. I don't want to catch a load of your buckshot in my backside."

With that caution, Slocum slipped into the shadows, moving quickly and quietly to flank the boy. He pulled back the hammer on the Colt and waited. In less than a minute he saw shadows moving within deeper shadows. The flash of a yellow bandana showed, and he knew he had spotted one of the highwaymen. Holding his breath, Slocum waited until the man worked his way past him, intent on the boy and oblivious to everything else.

Slocum brought the butt of his Colt down hard on the back of the man's head. He crumpled forward, unconscious. Slocum reholstered his pistol and took the fallen man's. No reason to let a good pistol go unused. It struck Slocum as justice to use Stockton's own man's gun and ammunition against the others.

"That you?" came a hoarse whisper.

"Course it is," Slocum whispered back. "Who'd'ya think it'd be? Clay Allison?"

He moved closer to the voice, which was now sounding uneasy. "Don't sound like you, Eddie."

Slocum spotted the man and moved quickly, bringing his left fist straight up in a short, hard jab that doubled the man over. Slocum cursed when the man's Remington discharged into the ground. With a backslap, he knocked the gun from the man's nerveless hand, making sure he didn't end up with a bullet in his guts. Slocum finished him off with a blow to the back of the head. Slocum added another gun to his arsenal, tucking this one into his belt.

The boy had said there might be four or five. Slocum moved around, heading away from where the boy held off the others. He wanted to find where they'd left their horses. With any luck, he could find out exactly how many guns he faced.

"One," Slocum said softly, seeing a gelding not three feet away when he rounded a bend in the trail. "There's two more. And a fourth." He quickly scouted and didn't find any more. "Only four. Good."

Slocum hurried back when he heard the boy's shotgun blast twice more. The boy had only two shells left. While he might have gotten both men going after him, Slocum didn't set much store in that notion. Stockton's men seemed cautious enough to avoid a wet-behind-the-ears boy armed with his daddy's shotgun.

Slocum's haste to see to Billy made him careless. He almost walked over one man on his way back to help the boy. For an instant, the man stared at Slocum, shocked that anyone else might be out this night. Then he came to his senses. Foot-long tongues of yellow-orange fire blasted from the pistol barrel as he fired repeatedly.

Slocum dived for cover, feeling hot bullet fragments creasing his arm and back.

"Jukie!" the man called out to his partner. "There's another one! Besides the kid, there's another one."

Jukie didn't answer directly. Billy's shotgun blast drowned out anything the man might have said. Pistol shots were his answer. The one Slocum faced was on his own.

Slocum pulled out the gun thrust into his belt and began circling, both guns ready. He rounded an upjut of rock and saw his target struggling to reload. Slocum began firing slowly, deliberately, aiming each shot the best he could. The man had a turn of luck when Slocum discovered the pistol firing low and to the right. Each round missed. When the Remington came up on an empty chamber, Slocum did a border shift, the empty gun going up and over while the one in his left hand came straight across, quick and hard.

The third shot from this gun found a fleshy target. The man grunted and twisted, dropping to his knees. He managed to get the cylinder back into his pistol, and fired. The shot went wild.

"Damn you!" he shrieked. The pistol wavered. Another shot burrowed its way into the ground at Slocum's feet. The man was bringing his gun up for another shot when Slocum centered him in his own sights. The pistol bucked hard in his hand. Another shot wasn't necessary. The man was almost lifted back to his feet. He fell backwards, body pinning his bent legs under him, arms outstretched on the ground.

Slocum took no chance as he advanced. He still had his Colt loaded and ready for action, in addition to the two rounds remaining in his captured gun. He kicked the fallen man's gun away, then checked for signs of life. Slocum's first bullet had caught him in the thigh. The second had damn near ripped out his throat.

Slocum shook his head. A hell of a way to die, just trying to rob a kid of a few dollars.

He picked up the fallen man's pistol and checked it. He hadn't been able to reload fully before Slocum got him. All the chambers held spent cartridges. Slocum tossed the gun away, as well as the one in his left hand. He'd have to make do with two shots in the captured pistol and the five in his Colt.

Another shotgun blast hurried him along. Billy had only one shell left.

"Give it up, Billy," came the remaining man's cry. Jukie, the dead man had called him. "Give us the money. Ain't worth dyin' over. No matter what Miz Romney's been tellin' you. She's a stupid old bitch. Don't die because of her."

"Don't say that about Mrs. Romney!" The boy jumped to his feet, shotgun to his shoulder. Slocum cursed. Jukie had been baiting the boy, and Billy rose to the insults.

The shotgun roared and the pattern missed Jukie by a country mile. The man grinned as he lifted his pistol for the killing shot. Slocum didn't have a clean target, but he couldn't wait for a better chance. The gun in his hand roared twice; the hammer fell on an empty third chamber. He threw the pistol away and whipped out his Colt.

Three more quick shots drove a confused Jukie back to the ground.

Slocum cursed. He hadn't even winged the son of a bitch and he had given away his most precious weapon: surprise.

Slocum cursed even more that he only had two rounds left. Reloading the percussion weapon would take too long, and he always carried the Colt with hammer resting on empty chamber. Out on the trail he didn't want to take a chance that the touchy cap might go off and send a bullet into his leg. Now he wished he'd taken the chance.

"Who the hell are you?" Jukie demanded.

"Leave the boy alone and maybe you won't end up like your friends."

"What?" Jukie roared. "You killed 'em?"

"As you told Billy, dying for a few no-good Reconstruction greenbacks isn't worth it."

"The others got what they deserved," Jukie said. Slocum heard the scrape of metal on metal. Jukie reloaded faster than he could ever hope to. Two shots. Slocum had to make them count.

"Blow his head off if he pokes it out, Billy!" Slocum called, knowing that the boy's shotgun was more useful as a club now that he'd run out of shells. It never hurt to keep the enemy guessing.

Slocum grunted when Jukie opened up on him. Whether the man had decided Billy was helpless or he just had a grudge against Slocum now didn't matter. Lead bounced off rocks and buried into pine trees. Slocum counted four shots, then went in. They were even now.

And Slocum had confidence. He'd been in worse spots than this. When he'd ridden with Quantrill he'd fought out of farmhouses entirely surrounded by Yankee soldiers using only guts and a couple of bullets—and, in those days, they usually had more guts than guns.

Slocum dodged behind a tree as Jukie fired again. The heavy *thunk!* told of the bullet splintering the tree trunk. Slocum saw his chance and took it. He spun around the tree, dropped into a crouch, and fired once, twice.

His insides turned to ice when he heard Jukie's harsh laugh. The man rose, lifted his pistol, then paused. For an instant, he stood as if confused and unsure of himself. Then he toppled forward, his pistol discharging into the ground. He lay unmoving.

"You got him, mister. You got the filthy backshooter!" Billy came up from behind, dragging his worthless shotgun behind him in the dirt. For a few seconds the boy's face lit up with the victory. Then he began to shake.

"It's all right, Billy. It's over."

"God, he's dead. I killed him!"

Slocum snorted. "You couldn't hit the broad side of a barn with that shotgun. I did the killing."

"If I'd given them what they wanted, they wouldn't be dead."

Slocum didn't say anything about the logic of that. If

Billy had given in to Stockton's men, they'd probably have killed him. Road agents, no matter how pure they claimed their motives, were murderers and no-account cheats.

"This Mrs. Romney. Is she in Durango?"

"Y-yes."

"Let's get you back to her and see what she says about all this. She sounds like a sensible woman. She your mother?"

"N-no. Sis and me board with her, kinda. Port Stockton killed our ma and pa a couple years back." When he spoke the words, Billy straightened. "They'd've killed me, wouldn't they? Just like Port killed my folks, they'd've killed me."

"Wouldn't bet against it," agreed Slocum.

"I don't want to stay here any longer."

"Should see to burying them," said Slocum, not looking forward to the chore. Then he realized two of the men weren't dead. Or he hadn't left them that way. He'd only slugged them.

"Never mind," Slocum said. "We'd better get moving. I'm going to take all four horses for my trouble. Mine has seen better days—quite a few years ago."

"Don't know where mine is," Billy said.

"All the more reason to take theirs." Slocum stopped and looked at the boy. About sixteen, he reckoned. A bit on the young side to be out alone with the likes of Ike Stockton roaming the countryside. But then, Slocum hadn't been much older when he had left to go to war.

The boy smiled weakly and thrust out his hand. "Thanks, mister. You saved my hide for sure. I'm Billy Burnham."

"Slocum. Now let's see if we can't get to Durango before more of Stockton's owlhoots run across us."

Slocum actually began to feel good about everything as he rode off on the gelding, trailing the swayback mare and two other horses. Life had taken him up and down recently. Coming into Colorado from New Mexico Territory seemed to change his luck for the better, even if he hadn't gotten away from the range war. He now had a good chance for getting away from it all. He rode along, head high, savoring the night breezes and the freedom of the Rockies. Billy Burnham brought up the rear, whistling tunelessly through his teeth.

Yes, Slocum thought, things were looking up. Sell the horses in Durango, and he'd have a good grubstake to reach Denver on.

4

Slocum had almost fallen asleep in the saddle by the time they reached the small town of Durango. He jerked erect, eyes blinking at the few lights shining in the mountain village. It took several seconds for him to realize that the lights were going out. The sun rose over the Rockies, giving warmth to a new day.

"You look dog-tired," said Billy Burnham. "Can't say I feel any better after all that's happened. Do appreciate what you done for me, Mr. Slocum."

"Need a place to stay," Slocum said. "Can you recommend one that won't steal me blind?"

"That's a poser," admitted Billy. The boy ran a grimy hand through his thin, sandy hair and finally came to a conclusion. "The West End Hotel's not due for opening for another month yet. If you only want a place to stay for a few hours, Mrs. Romney might let you bunk down in the back of the place."

"You never said what she did that she sends the likes of you on trips to Farmington."

"I'm a reporter, Mr. Slocum."

Slocum stared at the boy and tried not to laugh out loud. He'd seen a reporter or two in his day, and a sixteen-year-old didn't measure up to the demands of such a job.

"Well, not exactly," Billy said ruefully. "But Mrs. Romney says I will be if I do everything she says. I run errands and keep my eyes open. Learned to cipher and read and write pretty good. She lets me do up some of the obits." The boy smiled proudly. "That means writing up the pieces on the dead people."

"I know," Slocum said dryly.

Billy Burnham sobered. "There's been a whale of a lot of them lately. Too many. Been keeping me busy."

"I take it Mrs. Romney owns a newspaper."

"Yes, sir," Billy said, pride now entering his voice. "The best in the entire San Juan area. The *Durango Record*."

"Never heard of it," Slocum said. He had already lost interest in the boy's ambitions and how he idolized Mrs. Romney. All Slocum wanted was a place to sleep for a dozen hours, some hot food in his belly, the chance to sell the spare horses, and directions to Wolf Creek Pass.

"Better'n any of the others," the boy declared. "Better than the *Las Vegas Optic* or any of them other New Mexico papers."

"I doubt Mrs. Romney's got space for the likes of me. She have a stable for her animals?"

"Well, no. She runs a newspaper, not a livery."

"Then just point me in the direction of the stables and a cheap hotel." Looking up and down the dawnlit street, Slocum saw a variety of good-sized hotels, but none looked prosperous to him. In fact, the entire town of Durango didn't look too well off. Billy Burnham saw his expression.

"Whole town's been turned into an armed camp. Just like Farmington, except here they tend toward supportin' Ike Stockton. Didn't much like what the Farmington people did to Port Stockton." Billy spat at the mention of the name.

"But Stockton's men tried to drygulch you out on the road." Slocum didn't understand what was going on. "If you're from Durango and Durango is backing Stockton, why would his men . . . ?"

"Because," said Billy, "not *everybody* cottons to the way Stockton's been acting. Mrs. Romney is about the most outspoken. She says he's nothing but a common criminal and ought to be locked up. Don't make her too popular with some folks, but she don't care. She's got a mind of her own and she speaks it in the *Record*."

Slocum shook his head. It seemed that everything he did got him in deeper trouble. He'd almost been lynched by the vigilantes out of Farmington because they thought he was one of Stockton's men. He'd had that run-in with Stockton's men on the road and got the boy out of trouble, only to find they had returned to one of Stockton's strongholds. If the townspeople found out he'd killed two of Stockton's men and beat up another pair, Slocum doubted he'd escape the noose a second time.

The San Juan wasn't safe for him, no matter what side of the fence he was on.

"That one over there. How's it?"

Burnham shrugged. "Not too bad, I reckon. Caters to the likes of the railway men. Ever since General Palmer came in last year with the narrow-gauge we've been getting a lot of workers through that need places to stay."

"If it's good enough for General Palmer's men, it ought to be up to my standards."

"Yes, sir," Billy said. "Got to report back to Mrs. Romney, Mr. Slocum. Thanks." Billy thrust out a skinny hand.

Slocum solemnly shook it. "Any time, Billy. You keep out of Stockton's way, though. Can't rightly say I'd be around to help you with them a second time."

"Thanks again, Mr. Slocum."

Slocum watched Billy Burnham ride slowly down Durango's main street, turn left, and vanish from sight. He heaved a sigh of relief. Watching after anyone else got to be a chore. Slocum had troubles enough taking care of himself. Still, he was glad to have been of help to Billy Burnham. The more he heard and saw, the less Slocum liked Ike Stockton and his ways of doing business. Trying to rob and kill children didn't set well with him.

Slocum shrugged it off and rode slowly to the Palmer House. He dismounted, tethered his animals, and went inside—and found himself facing half a dozen levelled shotguns.

Slocum saw only fear etched on these men's frowning faces. He kept down his own fear and slowly walked to the registration desk as if the guns meant nothing to him.

"Want a room for a few hours. Need a bath. Somewhere to keep my horses."

"Mister, we don't let just anyone into Durango," said one of the men with a shotgun. He seemed confused that Slocum took such little notice of him and the other armed men.

"How much is the room?" Slocum asked the desk clerk. The mousy little man had turned whiter than flour. "Five dollars cover it? All I got're greenbacks." Slocum pulled out five battered one-dollar bills and spread them on the well-polished counter in front of him.

The clerk looked at the bills, then up at the man with the shotgun. He licked his lips, obviously desiring the money but fearing for his very life.

Two men came from outside and joined those already in

the lobby. One whispered at length with the leader.

"Go get Sheriff Watson. I think we got ourselves a horse thief on our hands."

"You think?" protested the man who'd brought in the information. "But one of them's Jukie's horse, and Jukie'd never let the likes of him come traipsin' in with his animal. He musta *killed* Jukie!"

"Get Sheriff Watson!" barked the leader. His finger tightened on the shotgun's trigger. Slocum lounged against the desk, outwardly calm. Inside, he seethed. Of all the hotels in Durango, he had to walk right into the one where Stockton's men hung around the lobby. Or maybe they were all this way. Billy had said Durango favored Stockton's position in the range war.

"You boys are getting riled over nothing," Slocum said. He carefully picked up the greenbacks. "Guess you're not wanting to rent me a room," he said to the clerk. He turned back to face the men with the shotguns. Only two of them had their weapons levelled at him.

Slocum made his move. If he waited for this Sheriff Watson to arrive, he might be dead. And even if Stockton's men let him live, he didn't want to stand trial for horse thieving and murder in a town not likely to listen to his side. This part of the country ran to vigilante committees and lynchings.

He'd already had a first-hand look at it.

With what appeared overt clumsiness, Slocum dropped the five greenbacks. The bills fluttered and got caught up on a gust of wind coming in through the hotel's opened front door. Slocum had sized up his opposition well. Their eyes followed the greenbacks to the floor.

Slocum kicked out and knocked away one shotgun barrel. The other he grabbed and twisted. When it discharged, the buckshot ripped away a portion of the wood counter. The desk clerk dived for cover, whimpering for someone to help him.

Slocum knew that he couldn't simply stand and wait for the other four in the room to decide to be heroes and use their shotguns on him. Slocum pushed hard, using the captive shotgun as a battering ram. The man holding it grunted and fell back into two others. Slocum swung the shotgun around and caught another in the knees. He toppled forward, screeching like a hoot owl. The confusion had reached the point where Slocum decided it was time to get out. A short punch sent the leader stumbling and Slocum took off, only to find the doorway blocked by a man wearing a corroded five-pointed star badge.

Slocum changed his direction, skidded around over threadbare carpeting, and hurried up the stairs to the second floor. Behind him he heard the sheriff yelling.

"There, there he goes!" cried one of those writhing around on the floor like a stepped-on snake. "He killed Jukie and stole his horse. Get him!"

Slocum got to the top of the stairs, considered drawing his Colt and opening fire. He discarded the idea as suicidal. The first hint of gunfire would convince everyone he was the enemy. They'd be more determined than a bloodhound on a scent.

Slocum kicked open the first door on his right and ran into the room. The window looked out over a narrow balcony with a low railing. He got the window open and slipped out onto the balcony, running along it to the front of the hotel. Below stood his horses, but Slocum saw no way of getting to them without being seen by those in the hotel lobby—and the men pouring into the street to see what the ruckus was.

He twisted around and saw a fancy piece of woodwork leading to the roof. Slocum went up it hand over hand, finding some support in a drainpipe. He flopped belly-first onto the roof just as the sheriff got onto the balcony below.

"Don't go running off and makin' it worse," Sheriff Watson shouted. "Get your ass back here so we can talk. Nobody's accusin' you of killing anybody."

Slocum wasn't buying any of that. The sheriff might have been an honest man—Slocum couldn't rightly say, one way or the other—but a lobby filled with Stockton's men didn't inspire much faith in any sheriff's ability to keep from standing back and watching a lynching.

He got to his feet, making his way along the sloping roof covered with the wood shingles. He heard the sheriff coming after him, but Slocum was determined not to be taken so easily. All he wanted was to get out of Durango in one piece.

His mind raced as he considered all the possibilities. It might not be possible to get back to his horses. If not, the Denver & Rio Grande Railway might get him up to Denver, if he could catch the narrow-gauge just as it was leaving. Otherwise, the sheriff would be sure to have a deputy or two, or an entire posse, waiting to check every passenger.

"Stop running, damn it!" came the cry from behind him. "I don't want to shoot you. I just want to talk."

Slocum considered his position. From the slanting rooftop he didn't have anywhere to go but down. The crowd in the street pretty well assured him a reception laced with hot lead if he took that route. Getting to an adjoining rooftop for escape didn't look promising, and he wasn't about to shoot it out with the sheriff unless things really went to hell and gone in a hurry.

He turned around on the roof and studied the man poised on the edge of the roof, precariously hanging onto the drainpipe and the wood facade. Sheriff Watson looked to be in his late forties, going bald and with more white than brown among the strands remaining. His weathered face looked like tanned leather and his pale blue eyes squinted over at Slocum. Nowhere did Slocum read the kind of cruelty or cunning he expected from a lawman in Stockton's hip pocket.

But he could be wrong.

Slocum made his decision. "You just want to talk? Then why the reception committee below with the shotguns?"

"Come on down. You don't have anything to fear from them." Sheriff Watson looked at Slocum, the whipsaw build, the dark hair, and the cold emerald eyes. He laughed without any humor. "Hell, you don't fear much of anything, unless I miss my bet. Get on over here and we can talk about this some."

Slocum nodded and edged back to where the sheriff hung. The man dropped on down to the small balcony. The people in the street milled around, one or two starting the inevitable mumbling. Slocum saw some of the men pulling out their shotguns and rifles. The sheriff bellowed, "Put those damned things away before you get yourselves hurt. Damn it, do as I say! Now!"

Slocum was happy to see that the crowd obeyed. The rifle sights went off him and the shotguns were lowered.

"Get on about your business," the sheriff called down. "You'd think you folks didn't have anything to do."

More grumbling, but the crowd slowly vanished until only a tight knot of men remained. Slocum couldn't help but see that these were the same ones who'd been gathered around in the Palmer House lobby.

All of them were Stockton's men.

Slocum stood on the balcony two paces from the sheriff. Those cold blue eyes worked up and down Slocum's frame. "No, you don't fear much of anything," Sheriff Watson said.

"Anybody with a lick of sense would be afraid of them." Slocum pointed to the crowd.

"Well, you might have a point. Ike's boys got their dander up. Don't know what set them off, but you seem to be the one they decided to pick on. Have to admit that does look like Jukie's horse. And the others? Where'd you get them?"

"The swayback's mine," Slocum said. "The others I just ... found. Wandering along the trail between here and Farmington."

"Just like that, eh?"

"Did help out Billy Burnham. Some road agents had him pinned down. Can't say for sure but those might be the road agents' horses."

"You leave any of these ... uh ... road agents dead?"

Slocum said nothing.

"Can't rightly see how one man could get the drop on four of Ike's boys. Unless he was *real* good." Sheriff Watson's eyes fixed on the worn ebony grip of Slocum's Colt. "You might be that good, from the look of you."

"Sheriff, where's this leading? I've been out on the trail all night long, I'm dog-tired, and I don't want any trouble. I just want to get on up to Denver and look for some work."

"Seems fair, but there's some problem with that." Sheriff Watson peered over the railing down into the street, where Stockton's men had begun whispering among themselves. Slocum had seen mobs forming before. This one would explode before he could convince the sheriff to let him keep on riding. Watson knew that, too.

"Let's get on over to my office. Might be quieter." Watson climbed back through the window ahead of Slocum, turning his back. Slocum also appreciated that the sheriff hadn't tried to take his Colt.

"What if there's trouble along the way?"

"Reckon that's my province, not yours," Sheriff Watson said. They went down the stairs, Slocum tensed and ready for anything. But the sheriff's presence dominated the crowd.

As Slocum had already seen, they were better at talk than at doing. They shouted at him and waved their fists, but not a one even made a motion toward drawing a pistol or cocking a carbine.

Slocum had pulled the thong off his Colt's hammer, but he didn't make any move toward the gun. Some of the men grabbed at him, but Sheriff Watson bellowed, "How many of you want me talking to Ike about what a herd of goddamn stupid jackasses you all are? You know Ike doesn't like to hear that."

To Slocum the sheriff said, "That always gets to 'em. Ike's got a tight control on them. Just like a trained hound. Got to keep 'em in line by appealing to that."

Sheriff Watson opened the door to the jail and Slocum slipped in, glad to be away from the crowd. Seated behind a rough wooden desk was a younger man, with coal-black hair and eyes to match. He half-rose, hand going for his gun, but Watson motioned him to his chair.

"This here's a friend of mine and Ike's. Also one of my deputies."

"Name's Sullivan," the seated man said, not offering his hand. "That *is* Jukie's horse out there. And two others belong to men with him out on the road to Durango. They was supposed to be patrolling along the Animas River to make sure Jeb Norton and his vigilantes don't sneak up on us from Farmington."

"I know why they were out there, and you know I don't much like the idea. Jeb's all right. Just gets a bit spooked at times." Watson went over to another chair and sank down into it, as if it hurt every joint in his body to relax.

"I don't have anything to do with politics," Slocum said. He wondered if he might not just get it all tattooed on his forehead for everyone to see: John Slocum wants nothing to do with politics in San Juan County.

"Those men outside are accusing you of drygulching four of Ike's men. Serious charges. And that one horse. Even I recognize it as belonging to Jukie Scott. Can't say I know any reason for Jukie to let his animal go runnin' around loose."

Slocum settled down, perched on the edge of the desk behind which Sullivan sat. The man glared at him, but it didn't have the feel of personal animosity. The man just seemed to dislike everyone, for no other reason than that they existed.

"You must be curious or you'd've thrown me behind bars by now. Or let the mob take me."

"Never do that. Let the mob have you, I mean. Can't let my job go that easy. I'm just looking for some answers."

The rapid click-click-click of heels across the wooden walk in front of the jail caught Slocum's attention. Sheriff Watson shifted so that his hand rested on the butt of his pistol. The sheriff relaxed when a woman barged into the office, her face all storm clouds and thunder.

"Sheriff Watson, what's the meaning of this? Is this the young man those hooligans tried to lynch? How *dare* you allow such a thing in Durango? In Durango, for Pete's sake!"

"Hello, Mrs. Romney," the sheriff said. "Nice day, isn't it?"

"Don't go 'nice daying' me, Sheriff. You're not letting Ike Stockton dictate to you now, are you?"

"Ike's not telling me what to do, Mrs. Romney. You know that."

"I know you favor that outlaw. You liked Port Stockton, too."

"Porter wasn't the scoundrel you made him out to be."

Slocum listened to the two of them argue back and forth. He watched the woman closely and liked what he saw. Mrs. Romney might have been fifty. She might have been sixty.

It was hard for Slocum to tell. She wore a plain gingham dress and her hair was pulled back in a severe bun, but her real beauty came out in her anger. Mrs. Romney almost glowed with the challenge of arguing with Sheriff Watson.

"Let me get this right, Mrs. Romney," said the sheriff. "You're vouching for this fellow?" The sheriff's eyes dropped to the worn handle of the Colt, then back to Slocum's cold eyes. "He's a hard one. And you're vouching for him?"

"He saved Billy from the bushwhackers Stockton put along the road."

"Might have to ask young Billy about that later," the sheriff said.

"Looks plain enough to me, Sheriff," Sullivan said, his mouth pulled into a thin line. "This son of a bitch—excuse my language, ma'am—upped and shot down some of Ike's best trailhands. Then he went and stole their horses." Sullivan spat, accurately hitting the brass spittoon at the corner of the room.

"That's an evil habit," muttered Mrs. Romney. Louder, she said, "I'm referring to groundless accusations. This gentleman is just passing through. Let him be on his way."

"Can't do that, ma'am," said the sheriff. Slocum wondered if the sheriff enjoyed these arguments with the newspaper editor as much as Mrs. Romney did. Both seemed friendly enough, and this sparring was just verbal claw-sharpening, nothing serious meant.

Slocum wished they'd not chosen him to fight over. He'd just as soon be on his way north. Or east. Or west.

"If you can't, then at least let him go free. You can't hold him in this pathetic excuse for a jail. It's not fit for man nor beast."

"I sort of enjoy it in here," Sheriff Watson said, smiling. "But you're right on one point, ma'am. Don't intend to hold—"

"Slocum," supplied Slocum.

"I don't intend to hold Mr. Slocum until I get solid evidence he's done something wrong. His story about finding the horses might be right. Your story that he was only defending young Billy Burnham might be true, too. Might even turn out he is a cold-blooded killer come to murder and rape our women."

"Can't be any worse than Ike Stockton," raged Mrs. Romney.

"Don't go leaving town, Mr. Slocum. I'm going to be looking into this matter a bit more."

Slocum hardly believed his ears. The sheriff wasn't going to lock him up.

"Thanks for your vote of confidence, Sheriff," he said.

"Nothing of the sort. Doubt you'll be getting far. Train's not due in for a day or two. By then this'll be settled one way or the other. And it's damn hard to walk out of Durango. Take a look at the mountains around us. Now get on out of here. I got some investigatin' to do."

Slocum held the door for Mrs. Romney. Outside he said, "Don't understand what Sheriff Watson meant about me not leaving. All he mentioned was train and foot."

"Unless you go stealing a horse, there's no other way out."

Mrs. Romney pointed across the street to the hitching post where Slocum had tethered his horses. They had all vanished.

The woman's hand on his arm held him back. "Don't get so riled about it. From what Billy said, you didn't exactly come by them honestly."

"The old swayback cost me sixty dollars in Farmington!"

"Just be glad they didn't try to lock you up—and that those owlhoots only took your horses. The entire town's walking around, hand on gun, ready to fire at shadows. Damn Ike Stockton!"

Slocum muttered to himself. With his horses gone, he

wasn't likely to leave Durango. If he stole a horse, the sheriff would know right away who'd done it and that Slocum wasn't the honest traveller he'd claimed. But Slocum found himself tossed on the horns of the dilemma. Sooner or later, one of Stockton's men would report in about the four out on the trail.

Lynched in Farmington or lynched in Durango—it didn't much matter; dead was dead.

"You look all tuckered out," Mrs. Romney said. "Why don't you come and rest up in the back room of the *Record?* Not offering you much, even if the *Record* is the best paper in town."

"You've done enough for me, ma'am. Can't impose."

"Won't hear of you going off. Come along, young man. There's a great deal I want to discuss with you. Yes, a great deal." A firm hand took Slocum's arm and guided him down the street to the main office of the *Durango Record*.

All the way, Slocum felt accusing eyes on him. He waited for the bullet that would blast his spine into a thousand pieces.

5

Slocum was so tired he barely remembered curling up in the back room of the *Durango Record* office amid the stacks of raw newsprint, cans of volatile thinner, and printer's ink. The thin pallet, hardly more than a blanket, surpassed the finest feather bed he'd ever stretched out on. Mrs. Romney showed him the room and he tumbled down asleep.

He became restless when his dreams turned into nightmares: unseen men shooting at him from ambush, lynch mobs after his hide, an immense Ike Stockton laughing and looming over him. Slocum awoke with a start, hand on the butt of his Colt.

For a few heart-stopping seconds, he thought he might still be dreaming. The woman bending over him had to be a dream. She was too beautiful for anything else. Then Slocum decided she had to be real. He'd been locked in the throes of a nightmare.

"I'm sorry, Mr. Slocum," she said, her voice soft and

caressing. "I didn't mean to wake you. I just wanted to make sure you had enough blankets."

"It is getting cold," Slocum said, pulling the threadbare blanket closer. He sat up and stared at the woman. She averted her blue eyes and looked at the floor.

"I didn't mean to intrude. Honestly. It's just that you were so good to my brother I wanted to see if I could repay the kindness."

"You're Billy's sister?" Slocum hadn't expected the skinny youth to have such a fine-looking sister. Auburn hair fell in soft waves around her shoulders, framing an oval face. A delicate nose just the right length, perfectly formed lips pouting the slightest amount, high cheekbones and a peaches-and-cream complexion bewitched Slocum. When those blue eyes turned back to him, he smiled.

"Rachel Burnham, sir," she said.

"Pleased to meet you." Their eyes locked, green and blue. Slocum silently reached out and took the extra blanket from Rachel's slender-fingered hands.

"I've got to get back to work," the woman said. "Mrs. Romney gets testy if Billy and I don't do our jobs."

"On the paper? What do you do?"

"I take care of the books, make sure the bills are paid." Rachel made a face. "I have to try to collect from our advertisers when they don't pay on time, which is often."

"I bet you do a fine job of getting them to pay," Slocum said. He couldn't imagine any man not doing anything this lovely woman asked.

"You're even kinder than Billy said. But I *do* have to leave." Rachel pulled her hand away from Slocum's, leaving only the blanket behind. She hurried from the room, giving him one quick, coy look before vanishing through the door.

Slocum settled back, throwing the blanket Rachel had brought over him. He drifted back to sleep, his dreams this time much nicer—and of Rachel Burnham.

• • •

"If I can't leave until Sheriff Watson decides how guilty I am, I'm going to need a job," Slocum said. "With those horses gone, my chance at grubstaking my trip up to Denver isn't all that good."

"Stockton's men took the horses. Even that swayback nag," declared Mrs. Romney. "But they only did it to make sure you wouldn't go running off."

Slocum said nothing to this. That was exactly what he wanted to do. He looked past Mrs. Romney to where Rachel Burnham labored over a large ledger book. But this enforced pause in his trip north had its compensations.

"It can't be long before the sheriff decides I did kill Stockton's men. If he favors Ike Stockton, he can't come to any other conclusion. They'll string me up for sure then."

"Not so fast, young man," Mrs. Romney said, slamming her hand down on a table. "Sheriff Watson's a good man. An honest lawman. You'd come to trial. No lynchings in Durango."

Slocum snorted. It hardly mattered if Stockton strung him up or had a jury rigged with his men on it, then strung him up. One was legal, but John Slocum ended up dead either way.

"You won't be railroaded, I guarantee that. Durango might be a hotbed of support for that hooligan Stockton, but there's enough honesty left so's we don't give him complete free rein."

"What's this range war all about?" Slocum asked. He figured the editor and publisher of the *Durango Record* would know, if anyone did. Being stuck in the middle as he was, Slocum figured learning as much about the issues as possible could only help him.

"Gets complicated," the woman allowed. Slocum noticed Rachel looked up from her work, smiled, and returned to her columns of numbers. "Has a lot to do with that murdering swine, Port Stockton."

"He got shot up in Farmington, didn't he?"

"More than that. Ike got Port out of jail a couple times, but Port was a no-good, worthless son of a bitch." Mrs. Romney snorted and bent to fumble around under the table. She came out with a small, clear glass bottle filled with amber fluid. "Grippe medicine," she explained, taking a healthy swig of the bourbon.

"There," Mrs. Romney said, recapping the bottle and sliding it into a pocket on her ink-stained apron. "But about Stockton. Ike and Port came up here from Cleburne, down in Texas. Should have kept them there, but after the War, a lot of the Johnny Rebs moved into the San Juan area. Most all were cattlemen, like the Stocktons. They started a good ranch over in Animas, back in '73. Times changed. General Palmer came in with his narrow-gauge and linked up to Denver and Salt Lake City."

"And with the railway came sodbusters," Slocum said, beginning to see the conflict.

"You got the players in this melodrama," declared Mrs. Romney. "Port shot up more'n one farm. Got him in trouble with the law so much, Ike gets the bright idea of making Port sheriff. The entire Animas area caught fire then. Farmers getting burned out, anybody who didn't salute the Stars and Bars being tarred and feathered."

"Why didn't the governor do something?"

"Governor Pitkin?" Mrs. Romney snorted derisively. "He and Governor Wallace down in New Mexico are more interested in feuding between themselves than in solving problems along in these parts. Let the entire San Juan basin go up in flames! Pitkin doesn't care."

"I ran into what they called Governor Wallace's militia, just outside Farmington."

"He sent them to keep Stockton in check. After Port got

himself killed down in New Mexico, Ike started sniping at more'n just a few sodbusters."

Slocum shook his head in disbelief. It sounded as if Ike Stockton had taken on the entire world. The governor of New Mexico wanted him, vigilantes in Farmington wanted him, the farmers a few miles east of Durango wanted his scalp. Ike had been a busy man.

"To make matters worse, the Utes are stealing horses worse than ever. You might be lucky Stockton's boys took your horses. If you'd headed up toward Ouray, the Utes might have taken a fancy to that remuda trailing along behind you."

"Hard to think of horse thieves as doing me a favor."

"Just pointing out what might have happened, Mr. Slocum."

Slocum started to speak, but jerked around when Rachel knocked over an ink bottle. It clattered to the floor, trailing sluggish india ink behind it. The woman stared at the doorway leading to the side street, eyes wide, one hand over her mouth.

"Afternoon, Mrs. Romney, Slocum," said Sheriff Watson. "How are you today, Miss Burnham?"

"Fine, thank you, Sheriff," Rachel answered. Her blue eyes turned into blue saucers as she looked from Watson to Slocum and back. She obviously expected the worst from this unannounced visit.

Slocum didn't know what to expect. He straightened, making sure his pistol wasn't too far away. From the tension in the sheriff's shoulders and upper body, the man looked ready for trouble. Slocum would give it to him, if necessary.

"Why don't you come in the front way, like a white man, Sheriff?" grumbled Mrs. Romney. "The *Record* is always ready to interview the lawmen in Durango. No need to go sneaking about and scaring us all. Unless that's what Ike wants from you these days."

"Well, ma'am," Sheriff Watson said, taking his hat in his hands. Slocum relaxed a mite. No man hung onto the brim of his dusty brown Stetson with both hands when he expected to be using his sixgun. "This isn't exactly a social call."

From the way he said it, Slocum guessed that Sheriff Watson made social calls to Mrs. Romney a great deal. The slight flush that rose to the woman's cheeks told him how right that guess was.

"Well, Sheriff, what is it? Don't keep us waiting. If it's good enough, I want it for the morning edition of the *Durango Record*."

"Found those four men of Stockton's." Sheriff Watson stared unblinkingly at Slocum, eyes appraising. Slocum returned the look. "Jukie Scott and the other three had run afoul of the Utes. All were skinned and scalped."

"You're sure of that?" Mrs. Romney wrote down the sheriff's words with quick, darting strokes of her pen. Slocum didn't doubt that it would appear with a banner headline.

"Can't be anything else. Sullivan went out and found them. He was hot for your blood, Mr. Slocum. Don't guess that comes as a surprise. He *wanted* proof you'd bushwhacked them."

"Must have been convincing the other way, eh, Sheriff?" Mrs. Romney asked, pen poised. She dipped it quickly when Sheriff Watson nodded.

"Had to be a raiding party of at least twenty. Unshod hooves. Sullivan trailed them damn near ten miles before he lost them. They were heading back toward their reservation."

"What's this really mean, Sheriff?" asked Slocum. "I told you those four were road agents trying to hold up Billy."

Rachel's attention perked up again at the mention of her brother. "I just took the horses I found running loose."

"Can't say that's the way it happened, but can't say it wasn't, either. Not now. I'll try to find the hombres that took your horse, Slocum, but the ones belonging to Jukie and the others, they were recognized. I have to assume you were being a good citizen and only wanted to return them to the next of kin."

"Possible," cut in Mrs. Romney, her pen scratching quickly over a blank page until it filled with tight, jagged-edged writing. "Slocum was looking for a reward, maybe."

"He was just being a good citizen," said Sheriff Watson. "I'll get your horse back so you can get on out of here." The man put on his hat and stared hard at Slocum. "Get my drift?"

"We both want the same thing, Sheriff," said Slocum. "For me to be in Denver as soon as possible. Just get my horse back."

"Until then," said Mrs. Romney, "Slocum's working here as a printer's devil."

"Are you, now?" The sheriff cocked an inquiring eyebrow upward.

"Don't have anything else to do, and Mrs. Romney was kind enough to offer room and board."

"Stay out of trouble." Sheriff Watson laughed harshly. "But that's not really likely, is it? Mrs. Romney here acts like a lightning rod for trouble."

The woman took three quick steps and took the sheriff by his arm and guided him back to the side door. They exchanged a few quiet words too low for Slocum to overhear. He was sure, though, that Rachel heard. She blushed and tried to look even more intent about her work on the ledger books.

Slocum had started to relax when the *Durango Record*'s

front window exploded, sending glass shards throughout the print shop. A rock bounced along and came to rest not two feet from where Rachel sat. The woman looked confused, not understanding what was happening.

The gunshots sent all four of them diving for the floor. Slocum found himself with gun drawn and his left arm protectively around Rachel's shoulders.

"What fool thing is this?" raged Sheriff Watson. The man struggled to his feet and duckwalked to the shattered window, peering out into the street. "Damn!" he muttered.

"Who's doing it?" demanded Mrs. Romney.

"Who else? That's Ike out there. He promised me he wouldn't do this. Damn his eyes!"

Sheriff Watson started to stand, only to be driven back down when a hail of bullets ripped into the *Durango Record* office. A mirror at the back of the room shattered.

"This isn't the first time Stockton's shot up the place," Mrs. Romney told Slocum. "I don't go along with much of what he tells others to do." She glared at the sheriff. The woman had a mind of her own. As if to prove this, she took out her liquor bottle and took two quick pulls from it.

"Mr. Slocum, don't," Rachel warned, when he started to go out the side door and into the alley. "Just let Stockton get it out of his system. He doesn't really hurt anyone. Or he hasn't yet," she amended as a bullet knocked a large splinter out of her desk. If Rachel had been seated there, she would have caught the bullet in the middle of her back. Slocum started to say something about Billy's story that Port Stockton had killed her mother and father, then thought better of it.

"Stay down," Slocum said, ignoring Rachel's pleas. He got to the side door and went out quickly, keeping low. When he reached the front and looked into the street, he frowned.

"Sheriff!" Slocum called out. "Are you sure those are Stockton's men? I recognize that one. The one with the gray Stetson. That's Jeb Norton, the leader of the Farmington vigilantes."

"Damn!" shouted Sheriff Watson. "It is."

The vigilantes took notice of the sheriff and sent a rain of lead in his direction, driving him back to find cover. Slocum started to take aim and fire, then changed his mind. Holstering his Colt, he crouched, waiting for the vigilante leader to come trotting by.

As Jeb Norton passed, Slocum rose and took three powerful steps forward, launching himself up and at the man. Slocum's strong arms closed over Norton's; the force of the impact knocked the rider out of the saddle. Slocum had to let the man fall, with the horse between them. The animal began neighing loudly and rearing. Slocum stepped away and let the horse race off.

"Slocum!" the fallen man cried. "You *were* with Stockton. We shoulda hanged you good and proper when we had the chance!"

Slocum didn't let Norton get his rifle swung around. A heavy boot knocked the rifle from the man's hands. Before Norton could get his pistol from the holster, Slocum had his Colt out and aimed at Norton's head. Even though it was only a .31 caliber, that bore looked big enough to run a train through.

"Go on, shoot!" shouted Norton. "But it won't do you or Ike Stockton any good. He's not going to get away with it this time. He's not!"

"I don't know what you're talking about," said Slocum. Then all conversation cut off when another of the vigilantes saw that Slocum had captured their leader and came riding up, sixgun blazing. Slocum grabbed Norton by the collar and dragged the struggling man toward the *Durango Record* office. He got covering fire from Sheriff Watson and tumbled into the print shop.

"Tell the sheriff what you told me out there," ordered Slocum. He crouched down and emptied the Colt Navy, then reloaded when the vigilantes retreated to the far end of town. Virtually every window sprouted rifle or shotgun muzzles now. Durango's main street became a gauntlet too dangerous for any to ride. The vigilantes gave up and rode toward the south, in the direction of Farmington.

"We won't let him get away with this outrage, Watson! We won't!"

"Shut your yap a minute, Jeb, and calm down." The sheriff peered out the window and saw only a tense emptiness. "Any trouble in sight, Slocum?"

"The only folks I see look like they belong here, Sheriff," answered Slocum.

"Mr. Slocum! Sheriff! Sis!" called out young Billy Burnham, sliding in the front door. "Are you all right? I saw 'em comin' but I couldn't get back in time to warn you. They got your deputy, Sheriff. Deputy Johnson! Took him away, bound up like a calf at brandin' time."

Slocum watched Sheriff Watson's face harden. The lawman turned to Norton and prodded him with the barrel of his gun. "You kidnapped Charlie Johnson? Why?"

"You know why," snapped Jeb Norton, sitting up and bracing his back against a bullet-riddled wall. "You know Stockton killed that railroad man over in Almargre."

"When?"

"April fourth," Norton said sarcastically. "As if you didn't already know."

"That was yesterday. Even if Stockton did do it—and I ain't saying he did or he didn't—why kidnap Charlie Johnson? He was out east looking for Utes then."

"So you say," Norton said, but the man's tone indicated

he wasn't quite sure why they had taken the deputy.

"He was over at Pagosa Springs," insisted the sheriff. "Yesterday. There's no way Charlie could have got down to Almargre and back in one day."

"They're gonna string him up," Norton said, "to teach Stockton a lesson."

"Some lesson," muttered Slocum. "Stretch an innocent man's neck to teach a snake in the grass a lesson. You fool! You're only making this worse. It's Stockton you want, not some deputy."

"Deputy Johnson backs up everything Stockton says, just like Watson does."

Slocum heard all the conviction go out of Norton's words. He said to the vigilante, "Where'd they take Johnson?"

"Outside town. Not far. They didn't want to take the chance of riding all the way back to Farmington with him. Stockton might be able to catch up with us, and we weren't ready for a full-scale war."

"You just shoot up Durango instead," snapped Mrs. Romney.

"On your feet," Slocum said, ignoring the others. He pulled Norton around and shoved him out into the street.

"Where do you think you're going, Slocum?" demanded the sheriff. "This man's my prisoner. If anything happens to Charlie, I want somebody to hang it on."

"You want a sacrifice, just like they do," shot back Slocum. "I want to stop this here and now."

"What are you going to do?" Sheriff Watson looked at Slocum, a puzzled expression on his face. "You're not going to get them to release Charlie. I know them too well for that."

"Release him in exchange for Norton!" cried Rachel. "No, Mr. Slocum, you can't try it. That'll be too dangerous." The auburn-haired woman started to rush forward, but her brother held her back.

"Unless you got a better idea, Sheriff, that's exactly what I'm going to do."

"It's going to be all right, Sis," Billy Burnham said. "Mr. Slocum knows what he's about."

Slocum snorted. He wished he had the confidence the boy did in what was going to happen. He shoved Norton toward the door, Sheriff Watson trailing along behind. No matter what happened, Slocum wanted to put an end to the sniping back and forth between Farmington and Durango. He just hoped that the attempt didn't mean more deaths—including his own.

6

"This isn't any of your concern, Slocum," Sheriff Watson said angrily. Slocum looked and saw what the man's problem was. They still stood in the doorway of the *Durango Record* and the sheriff felt his power being eroded away in front of Mrs. Romney. Whatever went on between the sheriff and the publisher of the paper went beyond simple friendship.

"I can handle this better, Sheriff," Slocum said. He took the man's arm and led him to one side where they could talk privately. Jeb Norton stood sullenly, glaring at both Slocum and Sheriff Watson. "Look, Sheriff, you can't get involved in this without causing a real ruckus," Slocum began. He felt the lawman's instinctive bristling.

"Why not? It's my job. You just butt out and let me do it."

"You want more trouble than you have now?" Slocum demanded. "You're the law around here. The people of Durango expect you to keep the peace."

"And I wouldn't be doing that job if I let you swap this man for my deputy. What would Charlie Johnson think if I didn't try to rescue him?"

"I see your point, but look at it another way. I'm a private citizen. If you, as sheriff of Durango, go hell-bent for leather into that posse from Farmington, it can only cause more friction between you and them. They'd have to get even. That makes the people of Durango all the more interested in getting even right back."

"So that's something I have to deal with. My job."

"Seems your job would be better served if you didn't get the Farmington posse riled up at all."

"Too late for that. They've kidnapped my deputy and they intend to string him up."

Slocum glanced over at Mrs. Romney, who stood studying the pair of them. The woman was a shrewd judge of character. Slocum almost wished he could have her talking to Sheriff Watson, but that wouldn't do at all. This was his duty and no one else's. And when he saw the expression on Rachel Burnham's face, he knew he had to do it all by himself.

"You're the authority around here. The Farmington men won't take kindly to any action of yours. It'll only be seen as provocation. Let me go—unofficial and on my own— and there won't be that reaction on their part. I can trade Jeb here for your deputy. That takes the sting out of it for them. They won't have to justify why they're returning home without stringing up anyone. The Durango *sheriff* won't be the one who's taken away their fun."

Slocum saw Sheriff Watson weakening. The sheriff didn't want to have to face a lynch mob on his own. What man would?

"You have till sundown, Slocum. If Charlie isn't back safe and sound by then, I'm holding you personally responsible."

Slocum snorted. This wasn't the way he'd have wanted it, but it was about all he could expect. Everyone in Durango and Farmington was on needles over Stockton and his ways.

"You don't have anything to worry about," Slocum assured him.

Slocum took Jeb Norton by the elbow and guided the man outside. The crowd gathered and Sheriff Watson had to clear the path for them out of town. Even the women seemed to want the smell of spilled blood in their nostrils. Slocum didn't much blame them. Having the Farmington posse come charging into town and shooting the place up on the pretext of looking for Ike Stockton didn't repair the bullet holes, the busted glass, or the hurt pride.

"Why are you doing this?" asked Jeb. "This isn't any of your fight. Or is it? Have you thrown in with Stockton?"

"I told you once that I didn't have anything to do with him. It was the truth then, and it still is. I only want out of the San Juan area. But they took my horse, tried to put me in jail, and have in general made life hell for me."

"So why get involved now?"

"I see it as my ticket north. I want to reach Denver before the whole area goes up in flames."

"A bit late for that. Stockton's made sure that things won't settle down till he's dead."

"The deputy being hanged won't help matters."

"Don't care what Sheriff Watson said. We think Johnson was in Almargre with Stockton when the railroad man was gunned down." Slocum noticed that Jeb's voice cracked a little. The man didn't actually believe this at all, but it made for good reasoning behind stringing up the deputy from the nearest tree.

"We'll track the posse down and make the exchange. You for Deputy Johnson. Nothing fancy, nothing tricky. I'm not in this to win friends—or to get myself killed."

"Sounds fair to me," Jeb said.

"Better be. You're the first one to die if anything goes wrong. They may get me and hang me alongside Johnson, but you won't see it. Remember that, Jeb."

Sheriff Watson had provided Slocum with a horse, probably his own, and Slocum rode out with the hankering to just keep on riding. Steal the horse, let Jeb Norton go, forget about Charlie Johnson. It would be so easy. Forget the entire San Juan range war and let these people come to their own solutions or go to hell in their own way.

Easy, simple, safe. But not John Slocum's way. He'd promised to try to dicker with the lynch mob. He had to now, since his word was his bond. He had damned few things left in the world, but his honor was one of them. Slocum didn't even want to think what Rachel Burnham's expression would be if he kept on riding. Why the woman's opinion meant anything to him was a mystery.

He also realized he didn't want to disappoint Mrs. Romney. The woman was a tough bird, hard as nails, probably a real hellion in her day. She wouldn't approve of any man who didn't at least try to keep his word. For her, if for no one else, and for himself, Slocum would see this through.

"There's the track," Jeb said, pointing. The early spring grasses had been crushed by the passage of a dozen shod horses. Slocum saw bright nicks in rock indicating recent passage, too. He nodded and pointed. They kept riding for another twenty minutes until they heard the whinnying of horses ahead.

"Don't even think of warning them," Slocum cautioned Jeb Norton. The man turned in the saddle and stared strangely at Slocum.

"What makes you think I'm not as sick of this as you are? I live here, for God's sake. Seeing my neighbors all het up and ready to stretch the necks of anyone they don't like doesn't set well with me. But I have to go along with it."

"You could fight them," Slocum said. But even as the

words came out of his mouth, he knew how hard that would be for Jeb. The man wasn't a fighter. He looked to be a storekeeper. The range war had enlisted improbable people on both sides.

"They got Clay Allison on their side. Stockton's a cold-blooded killer. His brother was, too. We're peaceable folks, usually. We got to fight or we die."

"Don't have to lynch innocent men."

"Remains to be seen if Charlie Johnson is innocent," Norton replied.

"I believe Sheriff Watson when he says his deputy was somewhere else."

"I do, too," Jeb said in a voice almost too low for Slocum to hear. He smiled a little, then settled down to face the task ahead. Jeb Norton was a good man. So was Sheriff Watson. If only they could have got together the entire matter of Ike Stockton and his depradations might have been worked out. But that didn't look too likely.

And it wasn't any of Slocum's business, anyway.

He studied the way the men in front of him had set up their camp. Slocum saw instantly that they didn't intend staying here. They'd found themselves a cottonwood tree with a limb at the right height, and that was their only concern. Charlie Johnson sat astride his horse, hands behind his back, looking scared.

Slocum didn't blame him. He'd been in the same position not too long ago, himself.

"Call to them," Slocum said to Jeb. "Let them know what's happening."

Jeb yelled out. He stopped when he heard the click of Slocum's Colt cocking.

"Tell them we want to make a swap. No damaged goods on either side is the only way this will happen."

"Pointing that at me doesn't do any good."

"Might convince them," Slocum said.

One of the posse members came over on foot and stood in front of Slocum's horse.

"You again?" the man said. "We shoulda hung you when we had the chance."

"You really don't want to string up anybody," Slocum told him. "Especially not if it means Jeb here gets a bullet in the head. We swap. Your prisoner for mine."

The man looked over apprehensively at Jeb Norton.

"Damn it," Jeb cried, "do as he says. Unless you want me ventilated."

"Jeb, they got their heart set on hanging the deputy."

"And I got my heart set on dandling my grandson on my knee."

"You ain't got a grandson, Jeb," the man said.

"Damn right I don't. But when Jenny and little Art and Frank grow up, they'll give me grandchildren. I want to see them. Do you understand?"

"Sure, Jeb, I know. But the boys..."

"Damn them all! Set the deputy free so this jackass will let me go!"

"Can we trust him?"

"Mister," Slocum cut in, "you can trust me to shoot him down if you so much as harm a hair on the lawman's head." Cold green eyes bored into the frightened messenger's eyes. He turned and ran like a rabbit back to the posse. Slocum saw several gesturing wildly, obviously not liking the idea. Finally, the messenger came back.

"We'll do it, Slocum, but we gotta have assurances that—"

"You got my word I'll shoot Jeb unless you release Johnson right now," Slocum interrupted. "Let the deputy ride out and I'll let Jeb do the same. They meet over at that stump. That's about halfway." He pointed out the stump he meant.

"Do it," Jeb said.

When the man ran back to the posse, Jeb asked Slocum, "You're going to go through with this? No tricks?"

"Sorry you have to ask," Slocum said.

"I apologize. You're one of the few honorable men around here."

"You're wrong. Seems this Stockton is one of the few dishonorable men." Slocum fell silent, then said, "Go on now. Ride out, slow-like. Stop at the stump and wait for the deputy. Then you just ride on."

"What happens then? They'll want to come after you. They'll catch you and hang the both of you."

Slocum only looked at Jeb Norton. The man curtly nodded, then put his heels to the horse's flanks. He rode slowly, waiting for the deputy, then rode slowly on to rejoin the Farmington posse.

When Deputy Johnson came even with Slocum, he blurted, "They'll be after us in a flash. We gotta ride back quick."

"Don't worry about it," Slocum said.

"Sheriff Watson? He got a posse waiting for us? We'll ambush those sons of bitches!"

"Nothing of the sort." Slocum saw Jeb Norton talking to the others. He had gotten himself back into command. The trade had gone smoothly and now there wouldn't be any reprisals.

He had been right about Jeb Norton. There were more honorable men involved in the San Juan War than anyone thought.

The deputy kept looking back over his shoulder until they were halfway back to Durango. Only then did he begin to relax.

"Reckon I ought to thank you, mister," Johnson said. "That was a fine thing you did, gettin' me away from that mob."

"Just doing a favor for a friend," Slocum said. But he

wasn't sure who that friend was. Sheriff Watson? Hardly. Mrs. Romney? Or was it Rachel Burnham?

"I didn't do nothing to cause them to string me up like they was plannin'," the man said.

"I know. Sheriff Watson vouched for you."

"Yeah, but he didn't . . ."

"His word's good enough. You don't have to say anything more about it," Slocum said. He hoped the deputy had the good sense to shut his mouth. If Sheriff Watson had lied, Slocum didn't want to know. And if he'd told the truth, Slocum had done what he had to do. Either way, the deed was done and he had to live with it.

"They're not going back to Farmington," Johnson said. "I overheard them. Said they were going to Animas City and try to find Stockton, now that they couldn't get him in Durango."

"None of my concern," Slocum said.

"But you helped me get away!" The deputy seemed incapable of understanding that Slocum wasn't devoted to any cause but was staying out of this. "You got to help Ike now. They'll find him and—"

"For all the trouble this Ike Stockton's caused me, I'm as like as not to hold the noose for them while they put his damned head in it," Slocum snapped.

The rest of the way back to Durango, they rode in stony silence. Slocum got the idea that the deputy didn't much like him, even if he had saved his hide.

"You can work here as long as you like. You earned the chance," Mrs. Romney said.

"Some chance, cleaning up the print shop," Slocum said. "But I owe you for the room and board. I'll stay on a day or two and work that off. By then, Sheriff Watson ought to have got my horse back." Slocum hadn't liked the idea of giving back the horse he'd ridden out on to save Charlie Johnson. The horse had an even gait, strong chest and legs, and had seemed to beg to leave the San Juan.

Slocum had given the horse back to Sheriff Watson. Again, he found himself on foot and no better off than he had been when he'd ridden into Durango.

"This is where the stories are breaking. You can read and write," the woman said, eyeing Slocum with her shrewd gaze. "I can tell. Might be you have a yen to be a reporter."

Slocum laughed. "Leave that to young Billy. I only want to get to Denver."

"Nothing there you can't find here. Maybe there's more here, Mr. Slocum," Rachel Burnham said.

"She might be right, Slocum," Mrs. Romney said. "Think it over. Glad to have you around. You showed you were handy when those Farmington hooligans came through and shot up the place."

Mrs. Romney went back to her copy work. Rachel took Slocum by the arm and guided him toward the back room. "I'll show you where you can start, Mr. Slocum."

Once the door closed and gave them some privacy, Rachel whirled around and into Slocum's arms. The man didn't know who was the more surprised, him or the girl.

"I ... I never threw myself at a man like that before, Mr. Slocum." Rachel smiled and dazzled Slocum. "John," she said in a lower, huskier voice, "I wanted to thank you for saving Billy's life ... and mine."

"Don't remember saving yours," he said, surprised.

"When the vigilantes were shooting up the shop. You saved me." Rachel moved closer, her lush body pressing into Slocum's hard, well-muscled body. She moved in a slow, seductive way. Slocum hadn't realized he'd saved Rachel from any such fate as she'd just described, but he wasn't going to argue with her.

All he could think about were the soft, warm blue eyes, the way her lustrous auburn hair fell in gentle cascades around her oval face, the slight pouting to her red, red lips.

He kissed her.

Rachel tensed for a moment, as if she hadn't expected this. Then she returned the kiss with more passion than Slocum imagined possible, even in a lovely woman like Rachel Burnham.

Their mouths met hungrily and Slocum felt himself responding. His hands rose and cupped Rachel's face. A small smile crept across her lips as she said, "You're so much like Luke. So much, so very much. Kiss me again, John."

"Who's Luke?" Slocum knew he shouldn't ask, but he had to. The woman had brought up the name and now he felt a small distance forming between them.

"We were going to be married. He . . . he died. An accident. He worked for Ike Stockton and was riding range. They think he got down to see after a cow and his horse kicked him. They found him a week later."

"I'm sorry," Slocum said, meaning it. Such a vital woman shouldn't have sorrow enter her life.

"Luke's gone. It's been almost a year and I've gotten used to him not being here." She pulled away, eyes cast down. In a voice almost too low for Slocum to hear, Rachel said, "I'm lying. I've never gotten over him. I loved him."

Her soft eyes rose again and locked with Slocum's. "I need you, John. Not as a replacement. No one can do that. But it's been so long for me. You make me feel good all over again. You make me know the feelings I had for Luke haven't all withered and died."

She kissed him again, all hesitation gone. Slowly, Rachel spun in the circle of his arms until she pressed her firm behind into his groin. The hardness there grew until it pained Slocum and excited Rachel even more.

"I want you to do it, John. I want it. I *need* it!"

She tipped her head back so that he could kiss her again. She laid her head on his shoulder, soft auburn hair floating over his shoulder. His hands moved of their own volition around her trim waist, pressing, touching, gliding. He worked up until he cupped her firm breasts through the front of her blouse. Rachel gasped and shoved backward even harder against him.

Slocum thought he would explode. When Rachel reached between them and began fumbling at his belt he knew he'd have to let her go. This was taking too long. It had been too long for him since he'd seen a woman, much less one as desirable as Rachel Burnham.

"No, John," she said. "I want to do it. But we've got so little time. Mrs. Romney wouldn't like it. Not in the back room of the print shop."

Slocum felt the woman's quick fingers at his gunbelt, at the buttons on his denims. His trousers dropped to a heap around his ankles.

"I need *this,*" Rachel declared, fingers tightening on the stalk of Slocum's manhood. She grasped the hot, hard cylinder of flesh and began moving her fingers up and down slowly, teasingly.

"Can't take more of that. Just can't. You're doing things to me, Rachel. Things I haven't felt in a long time."

She smiled, more a devil than an angel now. They both wanted the same thing. And both were determined to get it. Now.

Rachel turned her back to him again, this time bending forward and placing her hands on a crate. Slocum didn't have to ask what she wanted him to do. He drew his hands back along her sides, stroking until Rachel moaned softly. He lifted her long, dark skirt and pushed it aside, then worked down her frilly undergarments to expose twin moons of silky white flesh.

He caressed up and down the insides of her thighs until

the woman quivered like a leaf in a high wind. With one quick movement, he dragged his fingers over the dampness he found between her legs, then stepped forward.

Rachel gasped as his length pressed into the meaty crevice of her buttocks. Strong muscles clamped at him, stimulating them both. Slocum reached around their bodies until he again cupped the swollen mounds of her breasts. Through the fabric of her blouse he found the pulsing, hard nipples.

He squeezed down hard on them. Tiny trapped-animal moans came from the woman's mouth, and she began grinding her hips in a slow circular motion that caught at his erection and demanded more from it—much more.

"Please," she called out. "I want you, John. Don't deny me. Please don't!"

"I won't. Wouldn't think of it. Not now." He bent his knees slightly and felt the cold air gusting around his cock. This wouldn't do. Not at all.

Slocum worked forward along the wetness of Rachel's sex. He moved too slowly to suit her. She reached between her legs and securely grabbed him, pulling him into her. They both gasped with pleasure as he sank deep into her moist, clutching interior. Aroused womanflesh surrounded him, squeezed him, tormented him.

Slocum began to move. Slowly at first, then with a rising passion, he stroked back and forth. Rachel joined in the motion. Her buttocks pressed fervently into his groin and cushioned his forward thrusts. When she widened her stance, Slocum thought he was going to be swallowed whole by her.

Rachel reached back between her legs again, this time not to guide Slocum to his carnal target but to stroke and squeeze his balls. The pressures mounting within him were too much when she did this.

A powerful tide rose within him. But it was Rachel who

stiffened, gasped, and shoved herself back hard. The movement, the tight sheath of womanflesh around him, the feel of her butt pressing into him, all triggered Slocum's reaction. He grunted as he spilled his seed into her eagerly awaiting cavity.

Movement continued for several minutes longer, but both Slocum and Rachel were spent from frantic lovemaking. Rachel straightened and pulled down her skirts. She turned and smiled at him.

"Thank you, John."

"It's me who should be thanking you," he said. Then he laughed. "Let's both thank each other. Reckon we both liked it."

"A lot. I liked it a lot."

He started to say something more, but Mrs. Romney's voice from the front room broke the spell. Guiltily, he reached down and hoisted his trousers, fastening them quickly, hoping the owner of the paper wouldn't come into the back room and find him with his pants down.

Rachel made it worse, trying to help him. But Slocum didn't mind too much. And he didn't mind at all when Rachel gave him a quick kiss and a look that promised even more when they could be alone.

"That's one fine woman," he said, watching Rachel Burnham leave the back room. Then he decided he'd best get to work. The room needed cleaning—and he had to do something to get Rachel off his mind. Otherwise he'd go out front and take her again.

He didn't think Mrs. Romney would approve. Whistling, Slocum began sweeping the floor.

7

"You still around?" Crazy Matt asked Slocum.

"Seem to be. Didn't figure on being in Durango this long, but Sheriff Watson's not got my horse back yet." Slocum dropped into a chair beside the grizzled old man. Crazy Matt was a fixture along Durango's main street, sitting in a wooden chair, rocked back so that the front legs were inches off the sidewalk planking. He sat and watched and occasionally spat with uncanny accuracy, hitting a small tin can set beside him.

"Reckon it must be that filly keeping you around," the old man said. He spat, then fumbled in his pocket to pull out two pecans. He juggled them around, got them into the right position, and finally squeezed down slowly. Slocum heard the thin shells cracking.

Crazy Matt began tossing away the parts that weren't edible.

"Want a couple?" he asked. "Put these away last October

and been working on them all winter. Can't wait till a new crop gets in. These are turning bitter on me. That's what I get keepin' them in my pocket like I do." Matt looked down and laughed. "That sight oughta drive the ladies wild. Would, too, if I was thirty years younger."

Slocum took two medium-sized pecans and positioned them in his palm. An expert squeeze neatly popped open the shells. Crazy Matt nodded his approval.

"You know, Slocum, they call me Crazy Matt because all I do is set around and watch. Sometimes I make funny noises." He gurgled deep in his throat. "Don't mean nothing by it. Hard to swallow at times." He spat and rocked back, locking his feet behind the front legs of the rickety chair.

"Bet you see just about everything that happens in Durango," Slocum said.

"You got a lot to learn about talking to crazies," Crazy Matt said. "You're too direct. We're supposed to be coaxed for what you want. You want to know about Ike Stockton, you offer me a drink. You want to know about that lady friend of yours, you have to set and talk a spell to get me in the mood."

Slocum laughed. "Can't see why they call you crazy. You seem pretty down to earth to me."

"That ain't got nothing to do with it." He made a strange noise deep down in his chest and spat forth a mixture of brown chewing tobacco, black phlegm, and blood.

"Tuberculosis?"

"Reckon it might be. Don't worry me none. Been fighting it off and on for well nigh ten years. But the kids don't understand the noises I make to get it out of my lungs."

Slocum heard the wheezing and congestion, even sitting a few feet away.

"Can't say I do much to discourage the idea. People say things in front of me they wouldn't say in front of a sane man," Crazy Matt went on.

"Why are you telling me this?" Slocum asked, curious.

"Been watching you, Slocum. You're all right. Don't want you gettin' in over your head."

Slocum said nothing. Crazy Matt would get around to what he was talking about in his own time. Slocum worked on the meat in the pecans. If they'd turned bitter, he didn't find any of the tainted meat in his. He suspected the fault lay not in the pecans but in Crazy Matt. The old man's condition was advanced and he might not last out the summer. But if, as he'd claimed, he'd been afflicted for ten years, he might linger for another two or three. Slocum had seen men too ornery to die—or too tough. He thought Crazy Matt might be one of the latter.

"Don't mean this range war. Stockton's a bad hombre," the old man said, "but he won't hurt you none as long as you leave him be. This ain't your fight, after all." Crazy Matt cracked two more pecans and began worrying out the innards. He popped one into his mouth, chewed contentedly, spat, and kept chewing. Slocum marvelled at how the man kept it all straight inside his mouth. Crazy Matt seemed to have no trouble doing it.

"You're talking about the *Record,*" Slocum said. "Suppose you might even be talking about Rachel Burnham."

"You might not be in over your head, after all," Crazy Matt allowed. "But you're still in Durango. Not a good sign, no siree." He shook his shaggy head sadly. He reached into his pocket for another pair of pecans before speaking. "That Miss Rachel's the crazy one. Mrs. Romney is all right, but Miss Rachel has got her problems."

Crazy Matt cocked his head to one side and peered at Slocum through a half-closed, rheumy eye. He spat and said. "You don't believe me. You're thinkin' all those kids runnin' up and down the streets named me right. Maybe they did, maybe they didn't."

"What are you saying about Rachel?"

"Like a man who's direct. Surely do. Too many folks don't ever get around to what they want to say."

Slocum held down his rising temper. He knew what the old man was doing. Sooner or later, Crazy Matt would get around to telling him what was on his mind. It might take all day, or he might spit it out soon. Slocum wondered if it was worth the wait.

The more Slocum thought on it, the more he decided it was. Why else had he stayed in Durango other than Rachel Burnham? The woman appealed to him—more than just physical attraction, he had to admit. She was enough to make him think about staying in Durango, or maybe asking if she'd like to go with him up to Denver. It had been a long time since he'd felt anything more than passing lust for a woman. Rachel ignited fires he'd thought long dead, burned out by the War and Reconstruction and the ugliness that followed.

What Slocum couldn't figure out was why he thought the words of an old man who just sat and slowly died from consumption would be important to him. He had learned to trust his own feelings. Those feelings about Rachel Burnham were warm and real. Nothing Crazy Matt could say would change that.

"Now take Ike Stockton," Crazy Matt went on. "He's a mean cuss when he's crossed. Nobody looks to get Clay Allison involved like he's talkin' of doing if he's a peace-lovin' man. Anyway, me and Ike have always hit it off well. He'll set and talk your ear off. Hardly seems the kind, but he will. Been good to me."

"You know a lot of what's going on, then," Slocum said.

"Ike had a real yen for Miss Rachel," said Crazy Matt. "Doubt anybody but me even knows that. Me and Miss Rachel, of course."

Slocum's curiosity began to get the better of him. This

was none of his business, yet he had to know.

Crazy Matt saw the light coming into Slocum's green eyes. He smiled a bit, spat, and said, "Miss Rachel didn't want none of him. Even though Ike wasn't nowhere near as much a hell-raiser then as he is now, she cut him cold. Didn't have nothing to do with him, no sir."

"What didn't she like about him?"

"Looked wrong."

Slocum started to protest, then fell silent. It had been more than a week since he and Rachel had made love so hurriedly in the back room of Mrs. Romney's print shop, but the words Rachel had used still burned in his brain as if they'd been branded there. She had told him he looked like her dead lover, Luke.

"What about this Luke she was going to marry? The one who worked for Stockton?"

Crazy Matt tipped his head sideways and peered at Slocum. "She told you that, eh?"

"She lied?"

"Not exactly. Not what I'd call an outright lie. Luke was just one in a string of men. I do declare, they all looked as if they'd had the same mamma and poppa." Crazy Matt stared unblinkingly at Slocum and said, "They all looked exactly like you, Slocum. Tall, black hair, rangy, dangerous. Can't say if Luke had green eyes. Don't remember him that well."

"Rachel said he was riding range for Ike Stockton, got down to tend a cow in a bog, and got kicked in the head when his horse reared. You're saying there's another way it might have happened?"

"Think Luke might have just hightailed it off in the direction of Raton. Seems likely to me. Might have heard of work over there for that squatter fellow Coe. Then again, ol' Luke might have just taken off because of Miss Rachel."

"Why?"

"Yes sir, I *do* like a man who's direct," said Crazy Matt. "Shows you have things to do, places to see, and no time to waste on lollygaggin'. Not like an old galoot like me, settin' in the warm sun and waitin' to die. No sir, not a bit like it."

Slocum had to ask, "How many men has Rachel had? The ones who looked like me?"

"Can't say I was keeping a tally. Must have been four, five, even six, if you want to count yourself and Luke. Lost count a while back. All knocked out of the same mold, leastways as far as you look. Strange thing, too. Damn strange."

Slocum waited. Crazy Matt would get to giving the information eventually.

"Mrs. Romney—a fine woman, Mrs. Romney—commented on the way Miss Rachel's father looked. Dead quite a few years now. Damned if he didn't sound like a dead ringer for you, Slocum."

"You said Rachel's father died years ago? I'd got the impression her people had all died, except for Billy, recently, and that Mrs. Romney took her in."

"Been years. I been sittin' and spittin' for well nigh five years on this very spot. Reckon it must have been just before I got to Durango. That'd make it, lemme see"—Crazy Matt screwed his face in a parody of concentration— "seventy-six or thereabouts."

Slocum frowned. Maybe he'd assumed something that wasn't true. He would have to ask. In a roundabout fashion, though. He didn't want Rachel to think he was questioning her.

"Never seen her with another kind of man. Not a single one at all what didn't look like you. She likes the type, maybe." Crazy Matt spat and stared at Slocum. "Then again, maybe she don't."

Slocum stood. "Thanks for the pecans. Been since Texas since I had any that good."

"They came from down in the Mesilla Valley. Damn near Texas, these days," said Crazy Matt. "Nowhere near as good as the ones from over in the East Texas piney woods." Matt fumbled in his pocket and pulled out what appeared to be his last two. He silently handed them to Slocum.

"Thanks," Slocum said, sliding them into his pants pocket. He looked at the shells from the two he'd just finished, dropped the shells into Crazy Matt's makeshift spittoon, and started across the street, going to the *Durango Record* office. In the middle of the dusty street, he stopped and stood, listening hard. The pounding of hooves from the south side of town caught his attention.

"Hell," he muttered. That much commotion could only be caused by another vigilante group hell-bent for somewhere. The Farmington posse had gone back after he'd traded Jeb Norton for Sheriff Watson's deputy, but that was almost a week ago. In that time some hothead could have whipped them back into a lynching frenzy.

Slocum took the thong off the Colt's hammer. Five long strides brought him to the sidewalk in front of the *Durango Record* and the relative safety of a water barrel at the corner of the building. As the riders came into sight, he pulled out the pistol and waited.

He recognized several of them as being from prior posses, but they weren't looking to shoot up Durango this time. They rode, heads down, backs arched, horses straining to get them through the town and out to the east—east, toward Ike Stockton's spread at Animas City.

Slocum watched the last of the vigilantes vanish in a cloud of dust, reholstered his pistol, and went into the front office of the newspaper. Mrs. Romney stood at the newly replaced window staring intently after the riders.

"More trouble," she said in disgust. "Never seen a bunch

of men more inclined to get themselves and everyone else into hot water."

"They must be after Stockton. Heard he was back at his ranch."

"I also heard that Ike's been down raising a ruckus in New Mexico. Got Governor Wallace all hot and bothered again. Ike doesn't realize what he's doing to us. Won't be a building left standing in Durango that won't have a bullet hole in it."

"May not be many people without bullet holes in them," Slocum said.

"What do you think of this, John?" Mrs. Romney held out a freshly printed copy of the *Record*.

Slocum took it by the corners to keep from smearing the still-damp ink and quickly scanned the page.

"Seems strong. The editorial blames Ike Stockton for everything. You think that's wise, Mrs. Romney? Most of the people around here are on his side."

"Those jackasses from Farmington would never have gotten it into their heads to come through here like they do if it hadn't been for Ike. His brother was a no-account lying, murdering son of a bitch and deserved what he got. Ike's a better man, but he's letting Port's death do things to him. And he's bound and determined to get us all involved, whether we want it or not."

Slocum wasn't careful when he laid the paper on a slate table. The April 11 date rubbed off on his fingers, marking him. He idly wiped his hands over his denims.

"Reckon it's never easy being an editor."

"You have to tell it the way you see it," Mrs. Romney replied. "I see Ike as being at the center of all our trouble. He'll make them mad down in Santa Fe soon enough and then hell will break out. The Santa Fe Ring's been wanting control of the Maxwell Land Grant and Railway Company for years and won't rest till they get it."

Slocum started to tell the woman that politics meant nothing to him when the new front window shattered into a thousand pieces. A bullet whined angrily through the print shop and tore a long gash in the back wall. Slocum and Mrs. Romney dived for the floor at the same time.

"Damn it!" she cried. "Those bastards are back!"

Slocum wriggled to the broken window and peered into the street. It was even worse than he'd thought. Not only had the Farmington vigilantes returned, Ike Stockton's men had joined them. Both sides were bound and determined to make Durango their battleground.

"Stockton's men have staked out the hotel," Slocum said. "How hard will it be prying them out?"

"Won't be done without burning the hotel to the ground," Mrs. Romney said. "And Ike can't get to the Farmington posse without getting cut to ribbons. This is a Mexican standoff."

Slocum ducked another barrage of bullets. Plaster and wood splinters from the walls flew as the heavy lead blasted through just inches above his head. He started to rise up and return fire, then realized this would only add to the confusion. Neither side deliberately shot at the *Durango Record* office. These bullets were just the strays.

"Whole damn town's going to be dead after this. You!" the woman called, shouting to a man in the street. "What's the meaning of this outrage?"

"Mrs. Romney?" the man said, keeping low. He dived and snaked into the office. "They came after us. Found us just outside town and started shooting. We didn't have no choice but to shoot back. They'd've killed us all!"

"Jesse Price, you know better'n that," Mrs. Romney scolded. "There's no reason you couldn't have lost them in the hills. You know them like the back of your hand."

"Well," the man admitted, somewhat sheepishly, "Ike did tell us to shoot back if they showed their faces."

"Look what it's got us now." More poorly aimed leaden death crashed into the *Durango Record*'s walls, driving them for cover again. Slocum rolled onto his back and stared up at the ceiling, his thoughts not on the gunfight but on Rachel Burnham. She was supposed to be visiting a sick friend on a nearby spread. The bullets couldn't touch her. There wouldn't be any danger for her there.

Slocum found himself getting antsy wanting to find out, to make sure Rachel was safe.

"Jesse, you go tell them to stop this foolishness. I won't stand for it. Not in *my* town!"

"Yes, ma'am," he said, "but Ike did tell us to not let those bastards into our territory again without tryin' to send them back to where they came from."

Jesse Price snaked back, heading for the hotel to pass along Mrs. Romney's order to cease firing. They waited for ten minutes, then the gunfire from the hotel ceased.

"I still have some power in Durango," Mrs. Romney said proudly.

Slocum believed the worst was over and that order might be restored when the Farmington vigilantes set up a howl of rage and started shooting again. The men holed up in the hotel began to return fire, slowly at first, then with greater urgency, as if someone goaded them into deadly action.

Over the gunfire came a name shouted by both sides: Ike Stockton.

The man responsible for the San Juan basin range war had just ridden into town.

8

"That fool!" Mrs. Romney shouted. "He ought to have kept out of sight. Now there's no way in hell that anyone'll be able to stop the fighting." Slocum moved to a spot beside the woman, Colt in hand. He had to agree. From their vantage point they saw more of the gunfight than anyone either inside the hotel or outside.

He didn't count that as any advantage.

"Where's Sheriff Watson?" he asked. "He might not be able to stop this, but he can at least get them thinking about something else. He does know both sides, and both sides respect him."

"He and Sullivan went out late last night to track down a Ute raiding party. Thieving Indians took a string of horses from the Murchison place. The sheriff won't be back till nightfall. Maybe not until tomorrow morning."

Slocum risked another look at the fight. The only good thing about being pinned down inside the *Record* office was being with Mrs. Romney. She was like a spider in the middle of a web, each slender thread running to her another line of information. Without it, she'd have made a poor news-paper editor. Still, Slocum couldn't see what use he'd put this information to.

Sheriff Watson out of town with one of his deputies. Charlie Johnson was in town, but he wasn't likely to tangle with either Stockton or the Farmington vigilantes, especially not after they'd tried to string him up.

Slocum considered what he might do and saw that what-ever it was would have to be more than joining one side or the other. He risked his scalp sticking his head out of the office and peering down the street. A plan began to form. He crouched down and started out into the street, but Mrs. Romney restrained him.

"Let them fight it out, John. I don't want you getting killed."

"I don't intend to get shot," he said, "but the chances look better if someone stops them."

She tried to convince him, but Slocum had already slipped out and onto the sidewalk. No one spotted him. He duck-walked along until he came to the alley. There he straight-ened and made better time, reaching the stables. Several men sat around an overturned keg of nails and played cards, ignoring the gunfight going on down the street.

They looked up as Slocum came into the stable.

"Help you, Slocum?" asked the owner.

"Need some wet straw and a wagon to put it in."

The owner pointed to a dilapidated wagon out back. A pile of hay to one side was the best Slocum could hope for.

"Hey, what are you doin'?" the man shouted, getting up to see what Slocum was about.

"Need it," was all the explanation Slocum gave. He put his back into forking the hay onto the wagon. It wasn't wet and it would burn like a son of a bitch, but it would have to do.

The owner started to protest. Then he saw the expression on Slocum's face. He subsided, grumbling. Slocum got the hay loaded and spread over the wagon bed, then hitched up a team of horses. Whipping them, he got the horses moving until he drove up the next street over from the hotel. Slocum spun, got out a lucifer, and scratched it along the side of the wagon. It died out in a sudden gust of wind. Slocum cursed and fished out another. This one sputtered fitfully but kept burning.

Igniting the hay, he leaped from the wagon. It started sending sparks and black smoke high into the air. At the top of his lungs, Slocum yelled, *"Fire!"*

He tossed anything he could find onto the fire. Two saddle blankets and a canvas tarp joined the burning wagon bed. Another load of hay from beneath a hungry horse's nose. The animals whinnied and began their fear cries.

The gunfire slackened, then stopped. Those within the hotel didn't want to be burned down while inside, and those firing on them thought the town itself had caught fire. Slocum did everything he could to reinforce this misguided belief.

He ran around yelling, "Fire!" and motioning for Durango citizens to do likewise. Several tried to put out the blaze but Slocum backed them off with his pistol. By the time the wagon had burned down to springs and axle, the Farmington vigilantes had mounted and left town. Stockton and his men came out of the hotel, intent on finding the fire and helping fight it.

When Ike Stockton strutted down the street, he spotted Slocum instantly. The people had isolated Slocum, ringing him but no one going too close.

"You set fire to the wagon?" Stockton drawled. A heavy Texas accent marked his words. Slocum knew this wasn't unusual in this part of the San Juan. Most of the original settlers in the Sugarite area had come from Texas after the War.

"It scared off the posse," Slocum said, wary of Stockton. The man was half a head shorter, stockier, and carried himself as if he'd explode in all directions at the drop of a hat. Slocum didn't want to be on the receiving end if Stockton did lose control.

Stockton surprised him by throwing back his head and laughing heartily. "That was pure genius, mister. Thank you kindly." Stockton thrust out his hand. Slocum found himself shaking with him. "We got rid of those bastards for a while. We can regroup and head out after 'em, chase 'em all the way back to Farmington." An evil glint came to Stockton's dark eyes. "We can damn well burn down Farmington around their ears. Maybe that'd give them something to think about other than coming where they aren't wanted."

"Won't solve anything," Slocum said. "That'll only make them madder. You ought to try to work this out."

"What are you, one of them lily-white asses what don't want to fight?" Stockton's mood changed like a mild spring day beset by black thunderclouds. His hand drifted lower, toward his gun, toward the fight Slocum didn't want.

Stockton's attitude changed when he got a good look at Slocum. Even if Stockton had been blind, he could have seen this wasn't a man to back down from a fight. Every line of Slocum's face had been etched by hardship—and winning. Stockton relaxed a mite, then laughed again, the bad mood broken.

"Hell, we seen enough fighting for the day. Boys, let's get on out of here." To Slocum he said, "You want a job, mister, you got it. You have the look of a range rider to me."

"Done some in my day," Slocum admitted. "But I have a job."

"Not around here. I know all the owners of the spreads." Stockton's face clouded again. "You ain't with one of them sodbusters, are you? Don't care what you done for me. You throw in with them and I'll see you in hell!"

"My job's not with any of them."

"With the Bar F? The Rolling J? Where?"

Slocum saw the man was getting irritated. "Been working for Mrs. Romney." Slocum waited for the explosion, the hand flashing to the gun, the inevitable dangerous response. Slocum blinked twice when Stockton only laughed.

"Have it your way, mister. But you can do a lot worse than working for ol' Ike Stockton."

"They're comin' back, Ike," one of the men called. "Those bastards got about half a mile down the road, then turned around and came back."

"Didn't see enough smoke to show Durango was burning down, I reckon," the man said. "Let's ride. Back to Animas!"

Without a backward glance, Stockton mounted and rode out of Durango at the head of his men. Less than a minute later, the Farmington vigilantes came back through town at a dead gallop. Slocum stepped out of the street and watched them go. They didn't even slow as they tore after Stockton.

"This is the way it's going to be for a long time," Mrs. Romney said, coming to stand beside Slocum on the sidewalk. "They're both going to use Durango as their battleground."

"No damage this time," Slocum said.

"Some would say that."

Slocum spun and looked hard at the woman. "What does that mean?"

She silently led the way through an alley and back toward the *Record* office. A tight knot of men stood in front of the newspaper office. Slocum got a sinking feeling in his gut when he saw a pair of battered boots stained with tobacco juice poking out. He pushed through the crowd of men, Mrs. Romney following in his wake.

"Slocum," came the weak voice. A fit of coughing robbed Crazy Matt of anything else he wanted to say.

Slocum ripped open the man's shirt. A single bullet had found a berth in the man's chest. Slocum had seen worse and the victim had lived. But they'd all been in fair shape before being wounded. Crazy Matt had more than one foot in the grave. From the pink froth mixed with black tar oozing from the wound, Slocum guessed that the bullet had gone through a lung.

"Slocum," Crazy Matt said again, "damnedest thing is, don't even know who shot me. Might have been Stockton, maybe the Farmington varmints, maybe even one of them." His eyes rolled up to take in the crowd around them. Slocum started to tell the man to save his strength.

It no longer mattered. Crazy Matt coughed once more, choked, and died.

"No loss," one of the men gathered around said. "Could have been one of us."

Slocum wasn't even aware of Mrs. Romney's hand on his right arm as he reached for his Colt. He jerked free, balled his fist, and drove it square into the man's chin. Knocked to the ground, the man stared up at Slocum in surprise.

"Why the hell did you do that?" the fallen man demanded.

"John, let it be," Mrs. Romney said. "It's not worth it." She paused, then said, "Maybe it is. Matt was more a man than any ten of those ground-crawlers."

The crowd dispersed. Slocum heaved Matt's body over his shoulder and took him to the undertaker's office at the edge of town. What few dollars Slocum had accumulated went to buying a decent marker for the grave. He hadn't known Crazy Matt all that well, but he felt he owed him something. This was the least he could do. Slocum walked away, aware of the lump in his pocket from the two pecans.

"There's no need to work like a house afire, John," Mrs. Romney said. "You're acting like there's no tomorrow."

"For Durango there might not be."

"Been almost a week since Stockton and the Farmington boys shot the place up," the woman said. She leaned back in her chair and studied him. "Something's eating at you. What is it? Spit it out. Can't be old Matt dying. It was unfortunate, but nothing he wasn't ready for, him being like that and all."

"When will Governor Wallace send the militia to Durango? There's going to be three sides to the range war. Maybe four if Governor Pitkin decides to muster troops here."

"You been reading private letters, John?" Mrs. Romney sighed. "Hell, no, you been listening to Rachel. That girl'll be the death of me yet. She's not supposed to talk about what I find out. Doesn't do for a newspaper reporter to go blabbing all over, even if it's to the likes of you."

"Wallace demanded that Pitkin do something about Ike Stockton. He won't. He knows how powerful Ike is in this part of the country, and he doesn't want to take any chances that the Denver & Rio Grande Railway lines get cut. General Palmer spent too damn much putting it in."

"You make it sound cynical, John, like the politicians are interested only in money."

"They know what side their bread's buttered on," he answered. "The men down in Santa Fe want control of the Maxwell Land Grant and Railway Company. That's lure enough to tempt a saint."

"Owning most of northern New Mexico and a fair portion of Colorado is enough to tempt *me*," Mrs. Romney said, smiling. "But you're right. Wallace wants to keep the rest of the Santa Fe Ring happy. Joe Palen may be Chief Justice down in Santa Fe, but he's crookeder than a dog's hind leg."

"I already ran into some of Wallace's militia. They're no better than the boys riding out of Farmington. No uniforms to mark them as official, more interested in lynching than in keeping the peace. And now Wallace has given an order that will set the entire San Juan basin on fire."

"Can't figure it out myself," Mrs. Romney said. She eyed Slocum. He knew she was not stupid. She knew exactly what Governor Wallace had done—and why.

"Keeping peace 'along the San Juan River' is the way Wallace phrased it," Slocum said. "That keeps Pitkin off his neck because it might mean only in New Mexico. The governor can't complain about that. What can Wallace do if his militia commanders think it means all up and down the San Juan River and come tearing into Colorado and just happen to find Ike Stockton?"

"I knew the politics of it wouldn't be lost on you, John. Fact is, they weren't lost on Rachel, either. Surprised me, since I don't think of the girl as having that kind of sneaky mind. Might make a decent reporter of her after all, if she learns to keep her mouth shut. Even to the likes of you."

Mrs. Romney turned back to her work. Slocum finished his chores and went into the back room of the print shop, where he'd put a small cot. He dropped flat on the cot and stared up at the cracked plaster ceiling. A stray bullet had cut a gouge. He'd have to fix it one of these days. But there was no hurry.

Slocum frowned, lost in thought. No hurry, he'd been telling himself. That wasn't the way he'd felt when he first came to Durango. Billy Burnham had needed help and he'd given it to him. But Slocum wasn't so sure about what he was feeling for the boy's sister.

Rachel was a pretty one. But did he love her enough to settle down here? Did she love him enough to go with him to Denver, or wherever his wanderlust took him? He couldn't ask any woman to share the kind of life he'd been leading, but back in Calhoun County, Georgia, he'd been the best trapper in four counties and the finest hunter in the entire state. While his brother Robert had been the real farmer, Slocum was pretty fair at growing himself. Stockton might not like the sodbusters coming into what he considered cattle country—*his* cattle country—but that notion didn't bother Slocum.

This kind of thinking about settling down was alien to Slocum. The only way he'd kept from going as crazy as a bedbug was to keep moving. The law looked for him in some places. He could never go back to Georgia because of the carpetbagger judge and his hired gun. They'd come to steal Slocum's farm after the War. They'd got it, but not in the way they thought. Two graves on a lonely hill marked how they'd become one with the land. And this had made Slocum a wanted man. Killing a judge, even a Reconstruction judge in the South, wasn't the way to stay at peace in a community.

Since then he'd been as footloose as could be. What was it about Rachel that made him think of putting down roots?

His hand jerked to his pistol when he heard the floorboards creak slightly. Slocum relaxed when he saw the object of his thoughts slip through the door and close it behind her.

"John, I'm so glad I found you," Rachel said, almost out of breath.

Slocum thought the worst. "What's wrong?"

"Nothing," she said, giggling like a schoolgirl. "But it's been so long." She dropped down to her knees beside his cot and reached out for him. Quick fingers unfastened his fly and fumbled around inside.

"Only since last night," he said. Then he groaned. Rachel had found what she so eagerly sought. She moved closer, her breasts rubbing against his thigh. It didn't matter that they were both still clothed. He felt her excitement, the way her nipples hardened into pebbles. She took the tip of his cock into her mouth and began moving her rough pink tongue around in small, erotic circles.

Slocum stiffened. It felt damned good, what Rachel was doing to him, but he wanted to talk.

"Rachel, I want to talk with you. Just talk."

His words fell on deaf ears. She was too lost in the carnal paradise she found sprouting up between his legs. The woman's lips parted and circled the end of his manhood, then she began working her mouth hard against him. Pressures mounted inside Slocum's body, pressures he couldn't deny.

"Never mind talking," he said, leaning back to enjoy what she was doing to him. "Just keep on." He ran his fingers through her silky auburn hair, guiding her head in the movements he liked the best.

He grunted when her hot breath gusted around his erection and tickled down low. Rachel managed to pull from his trousers the fleshy sack containing his balls. She massaged them, teased them, turned them into a churning mass that actually pained Slocum.

When he erupted, it was a sensation unlike any he'd ever experienced. Rachel knew how to make him feel better than any other woman. He told her, not with words but with kisses.

And then, after a while, even this wasn't enough. They made love all afternoon long, Rachel with passion and Slocum with a sense of desperation. The entire country around them blazed with a range war. Such pleasant afternoons as this wouldn't be possible much longer.

9

"Came in over the telegraph," Mrs. Romney said. She silently handed the flimsy yellow page to Slocum. He looked up at her. She nodded. "I trust my source. Throckmorton down at the *Las Vegas Optic* wouldn't put something like this over the wires without a reason."

"No mistake, then," Slocum said.

"None. We should expect the first of Governor Wallace's militia to hit Durango in the next day or two. They went up to Raton hunting for Stockton and didn't find jackshit there. They've been riding in a criss-cross back and forth over the New Mexico–Colorado border ever since. They started to come into Colorado at La Veta Pass, changed their minds, and are coming on." The woman's language told Slocum how angry she'd become over this new indignity heaped on the community of Durango. Mrs. Romney was taking it personally, as if she rather than Stockton was the cause of the militia being sent out.

"What are we going to do?" asked Rachel. The woman put one hand to her swanlike throat. Agitated fingers tugged at a necklace until Slocum thought she'd break the slender gold chain holding it.

"Not much we can do, unless we want to take to the hills," Mrs. Romney said, her ire rising. "Right now, the Utes make that look mighty unattractive."

"We dig in and wait," said Slocum. "That's all we can do."

"There's more," Mrs. Romney said, as if finally making up her mind. "I've been writing editorials against Ike Stockton. The editorials are going to be aimed at Stockton *and* Lew Wallace now. That man can't just send his personal army into another territory any time he wants. By damn, I'll burn the tailfeathers off him for this. And I'll make that good-for-nothing governor of ours do something."

"Looks to be the first time if you succeed," Slocum said. "Pitkin doesn't get himself involved easily."

"Maybe you shouldn't," Rachel said, her voice small and frightened. "They might come after you for it. Ike's been talking a bunch, anyway. Says you're a menace to the town and you ought to be run out."

"Nobody's listening," Mrs. Romney said. "They know better. The *Record* is a part of this town. A necessary part. Without the *Durango Record* they'd all be dumber than they are, and they know it."

"Sheriff Watson's out after Utes again," Slocum said. "I heard that Sullivan had ridden to the south and that Charlie Johnson's been drinking more'n's good for him."

"He never got over nearly being strung up by the vigilantes." Mrs. Romney made a few futile marks on her copy of the new editorial, then chucked the pen into a small niche on her writing desk. "He'll snap out of it sooner or later. Don't know when it'll do any of us any good, though. A sheriff gone chasing redskins, a deputy off on a fool's errand, and the third lawman in these parts drunker than a skunk." Mrs. Romney snorted and shook her head.

"I'd better look to getting the windows boarded up," Slocum said. "No matter who gets to town first—Stockton, Farmington vigilantes, or New Mexico militia—they're going to shoot up the place."

"Do it," Mrs. Romney ordered. "See Gus over at the general store. Tell him you can draw on my account for anything you need." She sighed. "I was getting to enjoy the glass windows, too. Been a long time since I could sit at my desk and look out into the street."

Rachel touched Slocum's arm. He nodded and both of them left the *Record* office together. Once away from Mrs. Romney the woman said, "John, we've got to leave. We can't stay in Durango. They'll kill everyone here."

"Depends on who you mean by 'they,'" he answered. "Doubt if Stockton will kill very many. He's still got a fair amount of support from the townsfolk. Why, I can't say. The militiamen won't care and the vigilantes won't, either."

"None of them like what Mrs. Romney's saying in her editorials."

"That's one of the penalties for being a newswoman. Mrs. Romney knows she can't be popular—but she's telling the truth as she sees it. She's a woman of principle. I admire her for that."

"I admire her, too, but she'll get us all killed!"

Slocum almost asked Rachel to come with him to Denver on the next train out. Something held him back. Instead he said, "We've got to get to the store. I need more nails and some lumber to brace the boards already over the broken windows."

"Billy will come with me if I ask," Rachel said.

"Might be as well. Go on out to your friends' place and wait there."

"You wouldn't come with us?"

"I'm not leaving Mrs. Romney like that. She needs help."

"It's her fight, not yours."

Slocum nodded as Rachel went back inside. What Rachel said was true. Durango wasn't his home and he probably would never fit in with the people here. It would be too hard living in a place that treated men like Crazy Matt as they did, where the Ike Stocktons ran wild, where the law was impotent to do much about vigilantes raiding the heart of the town.

Maybe Rachel would go with him to Denver. Maybe she wouldn't. But before that could be talked out between them, he had to see to helping out Mrs. Romney. The woman deserved it. Courage, even out here on the frontier, was all too rare, and ought to be helped along whenever possible.

Slocum carried half a keg of nails on his shoulder as he returned to the office of the *Durango Record*. He dropped it to the dusty street when he saw the half-dozen horses tethered in front of the print shop. Instinct took over; he reached to his cross-draw holster and took off the hammer thong. A calmness settled over him, the calm he always felt before going into a fight.

Those horses carried Stockton brands.

Slocum didn't rush in foolishly. Nothing would be gained if he ended up dead, and it seemed important to keep Mrs. Romney out of trouble.

Mrs. Romney and Rachel.

He stared through the broken window of the *Record* and saw three men arrayed in a fan, Mrs. Romney at the center. Rachel Burnham stood to one side, her hand thrust into a desk drawer. Slocum knew Mrs. Romney kept an old black powder pistol in that drawer and that the pistol hadn't been fired in years. If Rachel tried to use it, the antique weapon might blow up in her hand. Or, worse, it could rile Stockton into doing something far worse. Slocum wanted to keep the lid on any further trouble, but he wasn't going to do it at the price of kissing Stockton's ass.

If there were only three inside the office, Slocum figured he might be able to handle them. His Colt Navy could get off a couple of shots before they'd know what was happening. With any kind of luck—or outright skill—Slocum could drill Stockton with the first shot. That ought to end matters once and for all.

Might even be the end of the San Juan War, Slocum thought.

He slipped inside, hand on his pistol. For a moment, Stockton and the two men with him didn't notice.

"... you're one hellacious bitch, I'll grant you that," Stockton told Mrs. Romney. "I admire spirit in a woman, but not when it's stirrin' up such a ruckus. You're gonna stop with those in*flam*matory editorials, aren't you, Mrs. Romney?"

"Ike Stockton, I'll do no such thing. How dare you even suggest that I compromise my principles! We got freedom of the press. I intend to keep telling things the way I see 'em. And I see *you* as the heart of a lot of misery. If you hadn't gone into Farmington and shot the place up, they'd never have formed a vigilante group to come after you."

Mrs. Romney took a deep breath and rushed on before Stockton could interrupt. "Furthermore, that lowlife Governor Wallace has sent militia after you. For God's sake, *militia!*"

The woman made it sound like a curse.

"They wouldn't a' took it into their pea brains if you hadn't kept hammerin' away with your newspaper. If you won't abide by my wishes for peace in Durango, Mrs. Romney, then it looks like the boys here're gonna have to make sure you don't do anything stupid."

"Touch one piece of newsprint, Ike Stockton, and I'll see you burn in hell!"

Stockton laughed. Slocum had heard its like before. Cole

Younger had developed quite a sense of humor and laughed whenever one of his cruel practical jokes caused intense pain. Ike Stockton was a man who enjoyed others' agony.

"Touch anything and I'll see daylight through your head," Slocum said in a quiet tone more menacing than if he had shouted.

For two quick heartbeats everyone in the room froze. Then one of Stockton's hired hands swung around, saw Slocum, and went for his gun. Slocum's Colt spat a foot-long tongue of fire and lead. The man jerked, bent double, and fell to his knees, clutching his belly.

"You son of a bitch!" yelled the other. "You gutshot him!"

"D-don't!" screeched Rachel. She had finally gotten the ungainly old black powder Remington out of the drawer and held it in shaking hands. Slocum felt more threatened by Rachel than he did by either Stockton or the man with him. He moved to one side to get out of her line of fire should her finger jerk back on the rusty trigger.

"Don't go messin' where you don't belong, boy," snapped Stockton. "This is between me and her."

"Reckon it's gone beyond that, Ike," Slocum said in a friendly voice. With the smoking pistol still in his hand, it made him seem even more a danger. The gunman with Stockton made a move for his pistol. Slocum shot him in the shoulder, spinning him around. A second bullet shattered the man's elbow as he kept trying to draw his six-shooter.

"You're a big man when you got the drop on us. Let's step out into the street and see what you're made of, boy. I don't think you got it in you to face me man to man. I think your spine's made of shit. You'll fold and end up beggin' me not to kill you."

Slocum shook his head. "You talk a good fight, Stockton. Don't press your luck. I might take you up on it."

Both Slocum and Stockton dived for the floor when the

Remington Rachel held scattered pieces of lead ball and wadding across the room. The man Slocum had shot twice had struggled to a sitting position, back against the front counter. While Slocum and Stockton argued, the man had tried to draw his pistol with his left hand.

He wouldn't try that again. Rachel had blown the top of his head off.

No one moved. The only sound after the echoes had died down was Rachel crying. She sobbed incoherently. Slocum frowned when he thought he heard through the woman's fright the name, "Luke!"

Mrs. Romney broke the silence by saying, "Put the gun down, child. There, there." Mrs. Romney took Rachel in her arms and cradled her, rocking her slowly from side to side.

"Get them out of here, Stockton," Slocum said. "If you ever come in here again, even to buy a paper, that'll be you on the floor."

Stockton started to say something, then bit down the words. Grunting, he pulled first one, then the other of his men from the *Durango Record*'s office. Out in the street, several more joined him, but the gunshots had drawn attention. A large crowd milled about. At the edge stood Deputy Johnson, his face florid and his eyes puffy. He'd been drinking heavily, but the sight of his battered star reflecting in the noonday light took the fight out of Stockton. The cattleman gestured and his trail hands mounted, the dead man draped over his saddle and the other Slocum had gutshot barely able to stay astride his horse.

Stockton's small band left Durango without further incident. But Slocum worried. Ike Stockton wasn't the kind to take such crushing defeat easily.

He returned to his chore of boarding up the *Durango Record*'s front windows, then went to see how Rachel fared.

•   •   •

"Sure is dark in here," Mrs. Romney said. The boards over
the windows had cut out the afternoon sun almost totally.
Only thin slivers of orange had come through, but that had
been an hour back. Twilight cloaked the town of Durango
and the people went about eating supper.

"You're the one who wanted them in place," Slocum
said. But he knew the woman wanted the boards nailed right
where they were. Rumors of New Mexico militia arriving
had been running wild through Durango all afternoon. Slocum hadn't cared much one way or the other. But if the
militia did arrive looking for Stockton, they wouldn't care
who got shot. That wasn't their way, from all he'd heard.
And Slocum found it hard to forget his first encounter with
the ragtag band down to the southeast of Farmington.

"Everybody's on edge. Can't blame them," the editor
said, going to the *Record*'s front door and peering into the
street. Only shadows danced along. No vigilantes. No militia. No Ike Stockton.

"Can't go on forever." Slocum picked at his teeth with
a splinter, then asked, "Rachel any better? She was surely
upset over shooting Stockton's hired hand."

Mrs. Romney whirled around. With a sharpness to her
voice that startled Slocum, she said, "It's none of your
business. You don't go bothering her now, hear?"

"Mrs. Romney," he said slowly, "Rachel is the one and
only reason I'm staying around here." Slocum fell silent as
he considered this. It wasn't the only reason, but it was the
foremost. "A swayback horse being stolen out from under
me is no reason to stay in Durango when the Denver & Rio
Grande comes through once a week. I've had two chances
to go on to Denver. Come Thursday, it'll be three."

"I'm sorry," the woman said. "It's just that I've gotten
protective of Rachel. She's had it hard, harder than most."

Slocum said nothing. He knew what it was like to lose

family, property, everything but dignity. Without dignity there wasn't anything. But it got lonely and cold, and wrapping yourself in honor didn't much help when bitter reality came crowding in.

"Maybe I'd better go check on her. She was sleeping peaceful enough, but I do worry." Mrs. Romney went toward the back of the print shop. Slocum had let Rachel take his cot rather than making her go to her and Billy's quarters in the small building out back.

Slocum waited for Mrs. Romney to return with a favorable report. Nothing. He turned, spat out the splinter, and peered into the gloomy print shop. He saw nothing but faint scraping sounds attracted his attention. He walked on cat feet back and pressed his ear against the door.

Without hesitating an instant longer, he kicked open the door, Colt levelled. He was in time to see Mrs. Romney's feet disappearing through the window. Slocum cursed and rushed around to the front of the office and into the street. Down the alley at the side he saw three men, one mounted and two on the ground. Both the men afoot struggled with captives.

Slocum fired one shot into the air. The darkness made it impossible for him to get a clean shot at any of the men. The last thing he wanted to do was hurt either Rachel or Mrs. Romney. The shot spooked the horses and made it harder for the men to control their victims.

Slocum sprinted and got to the mouth of the alley just as Mrs. Romney kicked out and connected with one man's kneecap. He yowled like a stuck pig and bent to grasp his injured leg.

Slocum had only a silhouette for a target. He fired. The muzzle flash illuminated the entire alley. He saw the shock on the man's face just before he toppled forward into the dust.

Rifle fire from the mounted man drove Slocum to the

ground. He heard muffled moans from Mrs. Romney. They'd gagged and bound her. Stockton's men managed to get her over the saddle of a spare horse. Slocum fired, hoping to hit a horse, but he waited too long out of fear. Killing Rachel would haunt him the rest of his days.

Mrs. Romney staggered forward and fell into his arms, gasping for breath. Slocum pulled the gag from her mouth.

"Rachel!" she cried. "They took Rachel!"

Slocum knew. And it made him mad, damned mad.

For this outrage, Ike Stockton would pay with his life.

10

"They kidnapped Rachel!" moaned Mrs. Romney. "Those good for nothing, lowlife sons of bitches!" She threw off the last of the ropes binding her and stamped on them, as if this would get back the girl.

"Stockton's men?"

"Who else?" the newspaperwoman snapped. "I didn't recognize them, but who else could it be? Especially after this afternoon. Ike doesn't take kindly to being abused like that. He looked bad in the eyes of his men. He had to do something to get even, or there'd be no holding back. He'd lose control and all hell would be loose."

Slocum went and examined the one horse that had stayed beside the *Record* building. The brand was Stockton's. While that didn't prove spit, Slocum knew it as good as meant Stockton had kidnapped Rachel.

"You going to get the sheriff?" Slocum asked.

"Hell, I got to. What else can I do? But Sheriff Watson

doesn't get back for another day or two, though, and the way Charlie Johnson's been actin', I'm not sure he's good for much of anything. This might drive him straight to the Palisades Saloon and he'd never show his face again."

The woman's tone told Slocum what she intended.

"You can't go after Rachel alone."

"Who says I am?" Mrs. Romney demanded.

"Won't do much good taking Billy along, either. He's not even dry behind the ears. Looks to be a good way of getting yourself killed. Billy and Rachel, too."

"So we wait for Sheriff Watson? Those owlhoots will be back to Animas City before sunrise. No way to ever pry them loose from Stockton's ranch. Not a one in that part of Colorado what'd so much as sneeze without Ike's say-so."

Slocum considered and came to a conclusion. "Don't bother going to Deputy Johnson about this. I'll take care of it." He smiled wryly. "Looks as if I got a horse again." He patted the sorrel on the neck. The horse jerked away, not wanting anyone but her owner to touch her. But Slocum persisted and the horse quieted.

"It'd be you against a whole ranch," said Mrs. Romney. "No good way of reaching Ike without all his boys finding out first."

"Don't need to get to Stockton. All I want is Rachel back, safe, untouched." His voice hardened when he thought about a gang of cowhands given free rein with a woman as beautiful as Rachel Burnham. "Where do you think they're most likely to take her? Straight to Stockton?"

"Slocum, they didn't want Rachel. They wanted me. I reckon they saw her and decided she was their reward. Ike probably never even mentioned her," Mrs. Romney shuddered. "After all, he was sweet on her once. I don't think he'd carry a grudge like that."

Slocum left Mrs. Romney standing in the darkened street and made a slow circuit around the *Record*. Here and there he saw piles of debris, all recent. Bits of wood and pulp paper from the print room had been piled along the back wall, just waiting for a spark to ignite it and reduce the newspaper to cinders.

Stockton meant business. Not only had he intended for his men to kidnap Mrs. Romney, he'd wanted them to burn the *Durango Record* to the ground.

Even worse, those men had failed. That would make them all the more likely to take their anger out on Rachel.

"I'm riding," Slocum said, rejoining Mrs. Romney in front of the *Record*. "No time to lose."

"Wait. Maybe you can get some of the others to go with you. They're changing their minds about Ike. Slowly, granted, but this will bring them all around when they think on it a mite more. I know them, Slocum. They're good people in Durango."

"I'm riding out now," he said. He put his heels to the horse's flanks and leaned toward the far end of town. The sorrel obeyed instantly. Whoever had trained her had done a good job. Slocum approved of their expertise, even if he didn't like what the horse's owner had been about to do.

Tracking proved harder than Slocum had thought. Not only was the ground rocky, the thin sliver of moon in the sky cast a wan light that confused rather than aided. Weak shadows darted about, causing him to start. When a gentle spring breeze kicked up, Slocum about decided to quit and wait for morning.

But as he rode slowly, he thought. About his life, about the emptiness of eternally drifting from one town to the next, never belonging to anyone or having anyone he could call his. Rachel offered that to him. He'd been with his share of women but none affected him quite like Rachel. Something about her made him feel protective, wanting to care for her no matter what.

Slocum frowned. Something else about Rachel bothered

him, though. When she'd shot the gunman in the *Durango Record* office, she'd cried out her former lover's name. And Crazy Matt had said the woman always sought out men who looked like the dead Luke—like Slocum.

He smiled in remembering the way she was with him, the eagerness, the lover's fire in her eyes, the ways she pleased him. Rachel was one hell of a woman. What had gone on before, with Luke, with her parents, was history. Slocum sought her out now to prevent her future from being blighted by Stockton's men.

Slocum rode along lost in his thoughts, not paying much attention to his surroundings. The faint swish of leather against leather gave him his only warning.

Instinct caused him to fall forward, rolling across the sorrel's neck to tumble to the hard ground. He landed on his back, the air almost gone from his lungs. He kept from gasping only through willpower.

It saved his life.

A Ute arrow had buried itself deep in the saddle where he'd been. If he hadn't gotten free when he did, that arrow would have found a home in his fleshy upper thigh.

Slocum quietly sucked in air and quelled the rebellion forming in his belly. A Ute raiding party meant nothing but trouble for him. What did it mean for the men who had kidnapped Rachel? If she fell into Ute hands, she might be better off dead.

Slocum strained and heard the soft rustle of moccasins on rock. Even in the faint light of the moon, he caught a gleam off a splash of white paint on one brave's cheek. The Indian moved carelessly, possibly thinking he had already killed Slocum.

Slocum rolled onto his belly, came to hands and knees, waited, heart thumping wildly, waited, waited—sprang.

Like a coiled spring unwinding, Slocum launched into the air and crashed hard into the Ute. Before the Ute brave knew what had happened, Slocum's arm snaked around his throat and began tightening. The Indian grunted. Slocum jerked harder and felt the life ebb from his would-be killer. Slocum picked up the Ute's fallen knife and used it to make sure he wouldn't have to worry about protecting his back.

A quick swipe of the bloody knife on the brave's leather shirt cleaned it. Then Slocum went hunting.

Three more Utes circled nervously, not certain what had happened. Slocum crouched on a boulder by the trail until the last of the trio passed by. The captured knife served him well. The remaining two whirled their horses in a tight circle. Slocum judged his chances, then gambled.

He howled as if all the demons of hell rode on his heels. The high-pitched shriek rose and quavered, broke, fell an octave, and started over again. Slocum didn't know if the Indians thought the ghosts of their long-dead ancestors stalked them or if a large posse rode down on them. Whichever it was, they jerked their horses back around and rode off at a breakneck pace.

Slocum watched them go, feeling curiously drained. No sense of triumph warmed him. They had been a diversion and had kept him off Rachel's trail.

Even worse, they might find the rest of their war party and return for him. Slocum didn't kid himself for one second that this was the main body of Ute warriors. These four hadn't been leading any captured ponies. From all that Sheriff Watson had said, the Utes were making life hell for everyone. Slocum didn't think he'd run into a group of inept horse thieves.

The rest of the Utes were out there, waiting, watching, ready to do to him what he'd already done to the two braves.

Slocum hurried on into the moonless night, the awful feeling inside that he wouldn't be able to find Rachel in time.

•   •   •

The eerie quiet just before sunrise told Slocum of predators waiting for their prey to go foraging, of wary victims trying to eat before the killing began. No birds chirped. The sky glowed an ominous gray and blood-red. Even the wind had died to little more than a whisper through the tall pines and leafing cottonwoods.

This stillness gave Slocum his first hint and his first chance to hope. He heard men cursing and the echoes of their horses as they worked up a draw.

He put heels to his sorrel and covered ground faster now. While the dark night had slowed him, it had affected the kidnappers, also. They might know where they went, but they had the same problems seeing. And Slocum had to hope that Rachel slowed them down.

He hoped that was so. Otherwise, he might have to face the fact that they'd killed her.

An indignant squeal, followed by the meaty sound of a hand hitting flesh sounded.

". . . two-bit whore," came part of what a man said. "Shut up or we'll shut you up for good."

Slocum hurried now. The men's tiredness and irritation came rising up like scum on a stock pond. It wouldn't be much longer before they made good on their threats.

Slocum found himself frustrated by a deep arroyo running between him and Stockton's men. He managed to get down one steep bank and had to restrain himself from whipping the horse into a gallop to make up the time lost. Slocum knew any sound now on his part would warn the men. He'd taken too long, being waylaid by the Utes, unable to see in the dark, not knowing the country.

"Steady," he said out loud. "You're letting this get to you. Calm down." He talked to himself like he would to a spooked animal. That he got so upset over Rachel's kidnapping told him more than simple words ever could. He cared for her, something that hadn't happened in a long, long time.

That might make the loss even greater.

He settled down into the emotionless state he always managed to find before going into battle. It hadn't paid for a sniper to be out shooting at Yankee officers with a shaky hand. Slocum had been one of the best when it came to steadily sighting in, letting out his breath as his finger squeezed back. He'd been able to do it throughout the War. He'd do it now.

An hour later, he gained the far side of the arroyo and found distinct marks on the trail where Stockton's men had passed. He even found a piece of Rachel's dress snagged on a mesquite. He hurried on, only to rein back when he heard sounds all too familiar, sounds left behind when he rode with Quantrill in Kansas.

A woman sobbed and men laughed. When Rachel let out a shriek of anguish, Slocum knew there'd be no quarter possible for the men who had kidnapped her.

He didn't hurry. If anything, he slowed. A mistake now meant more than death to both Rachel and himself. He tethered his sorrel on a clump of *chamisa* and drew forth the Remington sheathed on the right side. He levered a shell into the chamber. The harsh metallic click as it rammed home sounded a hundred times louder than it actually was.

Slocum didn't think any of the men would notice. They were too busy raping Rachel.

He walked forward in a half crouch, eyes darting left and right. He quickly found a spot high up in the rocks where he could see the small campfire burning brightly below. The cold false dawn had given way now to a real glow in the east. The dawning day was no warmer than the night it replaced.

Slocum spit on his finger, rubbed it in the dirt, and

transferred the dark speck to the silvery bead of the rifle's front sight. He didn't want the sunlight confusing him. Only then did Slocum turn his attention to the people below.

Scraps of Rachel's skirt were scattered around the fire. Stockton's men had torn off her clothing before pinning her buck naked to the ground. One man held each arm and leg while a fifth had his way with her. A sixth waited, his fly open and his hand fumbling around inside. Slocum heard the standing man complain, "Hurry it up. I can't wait much longer."

Slocum gave the standing man his wish. His finger slipped back slowly, evenly. The rifle bucked unexpectedly, and Slocum knew he'd hit his target. The man raping Rachel jerked upright, his spine shattered by the bullet. He flopped forward like a fish out of water.

Silence fell until Slocum's second shot knocked away a man holding down Rachel's right arm. This allowed the woman to flail about in the confusion.

In spite of himself and the cold rage he felt at what the men did to Rachel, he saw her naked limbs flashing in the new morning light and experienced a pang of desire for her. He remembered her eagerness and insatiable sexual appetites. To have this done to such a woman went beyond the bounds of propriety and honor. It violated the basic laws of nature.

Slocum got off a third shot, which knocked the leg out from under a man scrambling for cover.

"Rachel," he called out, "run!"

The woman sat up in the dust, a confused expression on her face. She was flushed and then seemed to understand what had happened to her. She clasped her arms across her chest to hide her breasts and closed her legs to keep the dark patch of fur there from probing eyes.

"Run, Rachel!" he shouted again. Slocum knew better

than to stay in one position. The four men below commanded more firepower than he did. With surprise gone,
he had to move faster, shoot straighter, and get into just the
right position if he wanted to walk away without new holes
in his hide.

He made his way down the hillside, abandoning high
ground for a thick-trunked juniper. From this vantage point,
Slocum commanded the area around the campfire. He heard
angry voices not fifty yards away. He allowed himself a
tiny smile. Stockton's men were still in disarray, blaming
each other for everything that went wrong.

When an incautious head poked up to do some scouting,
Slocum fired. He missed a clean shot, but the bullet hit the
rock and shattered tiny fragments into the man's eyes. He
howled in pain and ducked back. Slocum doubted that one
would make much fuss.

"Who the fuck are you?" called one man. "This ain't
your fight. Get the hell out of here and we'll forget we even
saw you."

Slocum didn't bother answering. He knew what would
happen if he was fool enough to believe the man. They'd
leave his body for the buzzards.

It wasn't going to be his body feeding the carrion eaters.
He peered out and saw that Rachel had gotten to hands and
knees and tried to piece together her skirt and blouse. Shock
had set in, he figured. She ought to know how dangerous
it was out in plain sight like that.

Slocum drew the men's fire by darting toward the campfire and diving, belly parallel to the ground. He hit hard
and raised a tiny cloud of dust around him. A rain of lead
cut through the air just inches above his head. It was dangerous exposing himself to fire like that, but he didn't want
one of those raping fools to get the idea of shooting Rachel.

"I can't see," the one moaned. "I'm blind!"

"Shut the fuck up," snapped the one Slocum pegged as the leader. "We got him. You hear that? We got you by the balls! Give it up!"

Slocum crawled on his belly until he got behind their saddles. These weren't the best protection, but they were good enough. He sighted, waited, and fired. Another man slumped forward, dead.

Three down, one wounded, two untouched.

"John?" Rachel said in a tiny voice. "Is that you, John? Why are they doing this to me? I didn't do anything to them. I never wanted them to d-d-do that to me!"

"Get down, Rachel, and keep quiet." Slocum motioned to the woman, who sat in the dust a few yards away. She hadn't taken cover. If they wanted to kill her, she was a perfect target.

"John!" She sounded so piteous that Slocum wanted to hold her in his arms, to comfort her. But he didn't dare. He had work to do.

He rolled onto his back, then his stomach, and a final time to his feet, running as hard as he could. The move took Stockton's men by surprise. They'd thought he would stay put and take potshots at them.

One rose up, pistol firing. Slocum went into the curious state he had experienced so many times before. The world dipped in molasses. Everyone and everything moved slow. Slocum struggled as if lead weights had been added to his arms and legs. His green eyes flashed here and there and his brain came up with all the right things to do, but he moved slow, so damned slow!

His rifle rose slowly, he cocked the Remington, he pulled the trigger. As if he had left his body and become a detached observer, he knew the rifle bucked hard and that the bullet flew accurately. Like a marionette with its strings clipped, the man Slocum fired at slumped bonelessly. No question existed that the man had died instantly.

"Rod, where are you, Rod?" called out the man Slocum had blinded. The man clawed at his eyes, screaming for his friend. Slocum guessed that the one he'd just killed was Rod.

"Get down, you jackass. He shot Rod. He . . ."

Slocum's rifle jammed as he tried to fire on the blinded man. He threw down the useless rifle and whipped out his Colt. The pistol cocked and fired three times before one .31 caliber bullet found its mark. The man who'd been blinded by the earlier bullet lay face down, his blood seeping into the thirsty dust.

Slocum saw that the man remaining, the leader, was the one he'd wounded in the leg. He wasn't going anywhere.

Slocum took the opportunity to get an arm around Rachel's bare shoulders and pull her to safety behind a few low scrub oaks to the left of the spot where she'd been raped. Slocum knelt down beside her and shook her hard enough to get her attention. The glassy-eyed stare vanished and fright replaced it. Slocum counted this as an improvement. He could talk to her now.

"I've got to finish off the last owlhoot. I want you to make your way up the side of the hill and hide in the rocks. When I'm finished with him, I'll come for you. Understand?"

Rachel nodded. Slocum studied her for a few seconds more, hurting for her and wishing there was something more that he could to.

"I'll take care of them. All of them," he said.

"Please don't leave me." She clutched for him, but he slipped back. With an adroit spin, Slocum moved toward the campfire, keeping low, circling around. The man with the bullet in his leg wasn't going very far. Except to hell.

Slocum moved to where he thought he could get a good

shot. Frowning, he scanned the entire area for some clue to where the man had gone. Slocum moved forward, every sense straining for scent or sound or sight. He went forward enough to see bloodstains low on the rock where the man had hidden. But of the man Slocum saw nothing.

He whirled around, Colt taking in the terrain, hungering for a target. It seemed impossible that the man had escaped so easily.

The instant Slocum had turned his back, he knew the answer. He heard sand whispering and the harsh grating of metal against stone. Before Slocum could turn back, a gun spat leaden death. A fiery streak parted Slocum's hair. He pitched forward, unmoving.

Slowly, painfully, the man brushed the sand from his clothing. He'd buried himself, hoping to trick Slocum. He'd succeeded. On a leg too weak to support him, the man hopped until he stumbled, finally crawling back to the campfire.

Of the woman they'd been raping he saw no trace, but that was all right. It would be too damned hard explaining it all to Ike Stockton. The man managed to get his saddle onto his horse. Pain contorting his features, he heaved himself into the saddle and headed the horse back toward Animas City and aid.

Stockton wasn't going to like the way this had turned out. Not one damn bit.

11

Slocum moaned, wondering how it was possible for his head to hurt so much. Yellow jackets buzzed and stung the insides of his eyelids and a smithy hammered away on horseshoes just behind. Worst of all had to be the searing pain that tried to split him in two.

He groaned louder when fingers lightly touched the top of his head.

"Either kill me or make it better," he said between lips that refused to work properly. As if his instructions had been heard, a jolt of agony lanced downward into his skull. Slocum got his eyes open to see that his head rested in Rachel's lap.

How being in such a heavenly spot could hurt like hell confused him.

"Are you all right? You gave me such a fright!"

"Damned if I'm all right," he said. He struggled to sit up, but the spinning world forced him back. He decided this might not be too bad. Might be darned good. He laid there staring up into her angelic face, her auburn hair cascading forward in gentle disarray. Dirt smudges on her cheeks made her look even prettier, he thought. But a wildness in her eyes robbed her of perfection.

Slowly, everything came back to him. The way Stockton's men had raped her. Him going after them. The one he couldn't find ambushing him.

"Where was that son of a bitch?" he asked. "The one who shot me."

"He . . . he was all covered with sand. I think he buried himself. When he came out from behind that rock, I hid. I'm sorry, John. I should have done something. But I couldn't!"

"It's all right," he said, meaning it. He couldn't expect the woman to be in her right mind after being kidnapped and raped. Still, it would've made him feel a world better if she'd blown the fucker out of the saddle with a well-placed bullet.

"He rode away and I couldn't stop him. I just hid and shook all over. I'm so ashamed of myself."

It was Slocum's turn to comfort Rachel. He held her in his arms, as much for support as comfort. The world whirled about in giddy circles but soon quieted. He kissed her. Rachel pulled away, then melted in his arms. Her vehemence surprised him. He'd intended this to be only a reassurance, a little peck to let her know that he cared and would help her. But it became so much more—and it was Rachel's doing. Their kiss deepened and they lay back in the dust, their troubles vanishing. Slocum broke off when he got an uneasy feeling of being watched.

He sat up and looked around. The sun rose well into the sky and illuminated the mountainous terrain. His sharp eyes saw nothing, but Slocum had come to develop a sixth sense that seldom failed him. He *felt* someone watching.

"Somebody's out there," he said. "We got to ride. Best

we get you back to Durango and let Mrs. Romney know you're not hurt." He looked at her closely to make sure this was true. Some women he'd seen who were raped never recovered. One he remembered from the War walked around as if her soul had fled, leaving behind only an animated body. Others took months to get back to normal—and then he wondered. And a few, damn few, managed to shrug it off and keep on as if nothing happened.

Rachel looked to be one of those.

"Stockton?" she said, her voice catching in her throat. "That man who escaped. He might have ridden to Animas and gotten Ike."

"Don't rightly know where we are, but I do know it's a piece over there. Take a good rider on a fresh horse most of the day from here. Wounded, the man couldn't make it any time soon." He kept scanning the hills, on the lookout for Utes. Slocum knew he ought to tell Rachel about his run-in with the raiding party, but she had gone through enough. To burden her with any further bad news might unhinge her.

"I should have stopped him. John, I'm sorry! I didn't!"

"There, there," he said, taking her in his arms. He wasn't used to comforting a woman. Not like this. "We had best be on our way. You can ride, can't you?"

"Yes," she said. The feral gleam in her eye startled Slocum. A solid core of—what?—burned inside this woman. He couldn't figure it out, but he guessed it had something to do with her former lover Luke. Or maybe her dead parents.

"Then let's be off. I don't want to take the trail straight back to Durango. Let's cut way south and curve around." He wanted to avoid the Utes. This might not work, but swinging down toward New Mexico Territory seemed the safest route. Even if they ran afoul of the vigilantes, this had to be better than a blood-crazed Ute warrior.

Slocum shook his head. Life had turned into an endless escape. No sooner had he gotten free of the New Mexico militia than he found himself with a rope around his neck, compliments of the Farmington vigilantes. Now he dodged both Utes and Stockton. Of the two, he wasn't sure that the Utes weren't the easier to deal with. All he'd done to them was kill a couple of braves.

Ike Stockton's injury went a lot deeper. He'd not only killed his men—something not bothering Ike unduly, Slocum figured—he had also hurt his pride. Mrs. Romney wasn't captured, the scathing editorials in the *Record* would continue, and Stockton's support in Durango would begin to fade.

It already had started a slow decline, Slocum knew. Stockton couldn't keep riding into the town and shooting it up and maintain any friendships there.

"Help me, will you, John?" Rachel clumsily dressed in clothing she found in one of the saddlebags. The man's red and black checked flannel shirt flapped around her slender body but did protect her from the cold better than her own tattered blouse. When she squirmed into trousers Slocum took off a dead man, he couldn't keep his eyes off her. In spite of their plight, Slocum felt himself hardening, lusting after her, wanting to feel Rachel's soft body struggling against his. She made it even worse by wriggling her pert behind in a way designed to give even a bronze statue an erection.

"There. Do I look presentable?" The coy smile she flashed him belied all Rachel had endured in the past few hours.

"You're beautiful," he said. "And we got to ride like the wind. To the south."

"Down toward the southern bend in the Denver & Rio Grande Railway?" she asked. "If you want to get on the train, isn't it closer to go to Pagosa Springs? That can't be more than ten, fifteen miles back toward Durango."

"We go south. Stockton won't be expecting that."

"Whatever you say, Luke."

Slocum started to correct her, then bit back the words. Her dead lover had looked like him. That's what Crazy Matt had said. Rachel had been through a lot. A slip shouldn't bother him too much.

But it did.

He saddled the horses and checked through the saddlebags for anything worth keeping. Everything else he discarded. He helped the woman into the saddle of a small mare and then climbed up on his sorrel. Leading two of the horses, he headed south, the sun hot on his left arm.

"Why are you taking those horses?" she asked.

"We can ride faster if we use them when our mounts tire," he said. "It's going to be a long day for us. Even longer for the horses."

"Just like the pony express," Rachel said, more to herself than to Slocum. "You can ride a long ways and no one can catch you."

He didn't tell her he'd used this very system for robbing banks. With some planning and horses waiting for him, he had robbed banks in Kansas and been in Idaho less than a week later, bone-tired, considerably richer, and without a posse hot on his trail.

They rode, Slocum finding himself the weaker of the pair. Rachel rode with back erect, eyes alert, and she even hummed quietly to herself as the day wore on. Slocum found it increasingly difficult to keep in the saddle. His head hurt like a son of a bitch and blood kept oozing from the bullet crease along the top of his skull. Flies buzzed and dipped into the sluggish trickle and made the wound itch. He tried riding with his hat on and with it off. It made little difference. One way he kept off the flies and let sweat sting the wound; the other exposed ragged flesh to hot sun and the insects.

By mid-afternoon, Slocum had to call a halt.

"Food. I need some food." What he needed more than anything else was a long rest. A few hours' sleep might take the edge off his fatigue, but he needed sleep to help heal his wound and replenish the energy he'd expended just staying alive.

"You look pale, John."

He noted she'd returned to calling him by his name. He liked it better than Luke, for many reasons.

He wobbled and slid down off his horse. "Got to rest. Dizzy."

"We should have cleaned the wound back at the campsite. Here, let me do it now. I don't know what I was thinking of then. Sit down and hold still."

The pain blasted into Slocum's skull. He might have passed out, or he might simply have slipped off into a deep sleep. When he awoke the sun had set behind the Continental Divide. He sat bolt upright, then regretted the sudden movement.

"Don't do that," Rachel chided. "You'll reopen the wound. It went deeper than I'd thought." She looked down at the ground and wrung her hands. "Actually, I didn't even look at it then. I'm sorry."

"We're safe now," he said, lying. "You deserved a mistake or two, considering all you'd been through."

"It might make me a better reporter," she said. "That's what I want to do. Mrs. Romney is giving me little jobs and when I learn enough, I can go on to do some of the editorials, just like she does."

"What about your brother? He want to be a reporter, too?"

"No, Billy's got it into his head to go on up to Denver. But deep down I think he wants to work on the *Durango Record* as much as I do."

"You respect Mrs. Romney a great deal, don't you?"

"She took us in when no one else would. Ma and Pa got killed and we might have starved except for Mrs. Romney. I love her like a mother now. And I surely do respect her. She knows the newspaper business better'n any man in these parts."

"When did she take you in?"

Rachel ignored him, gently stroking over his forehead. Her dancing fingers outlined the bloody crease in his scalp and made some of the hurt go away.

"You want to camp here, John? I can't say we've gone more than ten, fifteen miles. If Stockton came back looking for the campsite, he wouldn't have any trouble catching up with us."

Slocum cursed his weakness. He had thought Rachel would hold them up, but it had turned out the other way. She had ridden with the best while he had almost fainted in the saddle.

"We got to make some more distance," he said. Teeth set, he got to his feet, pushing Rachel away. He didn't mind her touch; he just wanted to be sure he could walk on his own.

"What's that? Thunder?" Rachel asked, tipping her head to one side and listening hard.

"Hoofbeats," he said. Slocum decided the sounds came from the south, toward New Mexico. He frowned. That many riders coming from the south didn't make any sense. All reports had the Utes to the north and west. If Stockton came up on them, it'd be from the east.

"I'm going scouting. You stay here and wait for me."

"John," she said, her voice almost too low to hear. "What if you don't come back?"

Slocum held back a flare of anger. "I'm not running out on you."

"I . . . I know that. But so many others I've loved have

gone off and never come back."

"I'll be back," he assured her. Rachel stood and let him kiss her. No passion came with the kiss. Slocum swung into the saddle and held on for dear life. Riding along at a good pace, the wind in his face and the sun warming him, Slocum felt strength pouring back into him. By the time he reached the notch that spread out to overlook a fan-shaped valley dotted with the colors of a new spring, he knew he could lick his weight in wildcats.

He rose in the stirrups and peered into the sun at the neat column of men riding along behind the rippling banner. Definitely military, he decided. No one else went out with such precision. He decided to let them ride on but the sun betrayed him. A silver conch on the saddle reflected and caught the attention of the officer in the lead. The distant officer held up a hand and turned the column.

Can't be too bad, he thought. *They're wearing uniforms. The last militia I ran into didn't.*

Slocum sat, leg curled around his saddlehorn as he waited. The officer halted the column of twenty men a dozen yards away. He said something to the sergeant and then rode forward slowly. Slocum noticed that the officer had pulled free the flap of his holster to reveal the butt of his pistol. He expected trouble.

"Afternoon, Captain," Slocum called out.

"Who are you?" the officer demanded harshly.

"Yes, sure is a nice day," said Slocum.

"I asked a question, mister." The officer went for his pistol. Slocum's Colt Navy slid free of its holster and centered on the officer's chest.

"Don't get any ideas, Captain. I'm not in the mood for trouble."

"My sergeant will see you in front of a firing squad if you harm me."

"That may be true," Slocum allowed, "but *you* won't be around to see it. Now, neither of us want that. Let's talk this out and we can both ride away."

"You're one of Stockton's men." The captain made it sound like a curse. From Slocum's point of view, it was.

"No love lost between me and Ike Stockton," Slocum said. "Fact is, I'm riding south to avoid him. Who are you?"

"Captain Wilbur O'Malley, New Mexico militia."

"You're a regular. What brings you to this part of Colorado?"

"I'm under the direct command of General Frost." The captain apparently thought that was all the explanation needed. When Slocum said nothing, the officer added, "General Frost has been ordered by Governor Wallace to maintain civil order along the San Juan."

"You're a ways from the San Juan River. And you must be twenty, thirty miles north of San Juan County down in New Mexico." Slocum didn't like the idea of one territory's militia blundering into another jurisdiction. He squinted when he decided that Captain O'Malley wasn't the blundering kind. He had entered Colorado knowing full well where he rode.

"I was ordered to keep order along the San Juan." The words came flat, harsh. "You have not answered my question, sir."

"Name's John Slocum." Slocum held back giving any details to this man. "I'm riding south a ways, then going on to Durango."

"That's out of your way."

"Utes," Slocum explained. "Between here and Durango must be damn near a dozen Ute raiding parties. This way's safer."

"You don't look to be the kind to run from a fight."

Slocum shrugged. "Can't abide by killing." To this, the

captain laughed without any trace of humor. Slocum joined in. He still held his Colt levelled on the officer.

He put away his Colt and rocked back in the saddle. "Sheriff Watson from over in Durango is responsible for keeping the peace in this part of the country. He know you're intruding?"

"I am following orders given me by—"

"General Frost, acting on orders from Lew Wallace. You said that."

"I find your manner offensive, Mr. Slocum. Please accompany me back to the column. We will escort you as far as Vermejo."

"Don't think so," Socum cut in. "That's out of my way. I'm going in the other direction. To Durango."

"You have no choice. Since Governor Pitkin saw fit to ignore Governor Wallace's plea to turn over Ike Stockton— or at least stop his depradations—we will maintain order, at any cost."

"I'm not disturbing anything. I don't have any special liking for Stockton, and I just intend to get out of the San Juan as fast as I can."

"Then you will find Vermejo a pleasant diversion."

"You're not listening, Captain." Slocum's ears pricked up when he heard the sergeant giving quiet commands. The words vanished in the distance, but the cocking of carbines from the front of the column sounded with deadly intent. If he didn't obey the officer's orders, the troopers would shoot Slocum down.

Slocum considered his dilemma, then acted without consciously coming to a conclusion. His Colt came out and a bullet ricocheted off the rocks just inches in front of Captain O'Malley's horse. The animal spooked, just as Slocum had known it would. Rearing, the horse almost threw its rider. The officer hung on with grim determination, but as he spun around on the bucking horse, he shielded Slocum from direct fire.

Slocum dropped his feet to their stirrups and rode low, kicking hard into the sorrel's flanks. The horse responded like a champion. The few rifle shots seeking Slocum's flesh went wide. He stayed low and rode for a cluster of juniper. Behind the shielding trees, Slocum chanced a quick backward glance.

"Damn," he said with feeling. Captain O'Malley had calmed his bucking horse and regained enough composure to order his column forward. Slocum didn't see much chance of escaping twenty troopers.

But he'd try. He couldn't leave Rachel on her own, not with Ike Stockton coming after her. Even worse was the promise he'd given her before he left. She feared she'd never see him again, that he would vanish as the others in her life had vanished. He'd given his word he would return. And return he would.

How, Slocum didn't know, but he would. He worked to remember the country he had ridden through, then smiled. It would be a desperate attempt, but Slocum knew it would work. It had to.

He rode up an arroyo, away from the vantage point at the notch leading out into the valley. The mountains rose up on either side with startling rapidity as the ground sloped upward to the north. Slocum had come this way, but he didn't retrace his trail. To do that meant the militia would overtake him before he got a mile.

He rode off to the west, found the mouth of the canyon, and entered without hesitation. He had ridden the rim of this canyon and knew it ended in a box less than a mile in. From behind, a small cry went up as the troopers recognized the terrain and thought he doomed himself.

The captain stationed a few of his men at the mouth.

The rest, under his leadership, hurried after Slocum.

"This had better work," Slocum said to the horse. "Hate to do it. I really do." He patted the horse on the neck, wishing he could think of some way to keep her. The animal had served him well—and if his plan worked, the sorrel would continue serving him long after they parted company.

"After him!" came the cry echoing up the canyon. "One dollar bonus to the man who sights him first!"

For heady reward like that, Slocum figured the troopers would fall all over themselves seeking him out. Captain O'Malley would soon realize that the reward he placed on Slocum's head was far too small. He laughed to himself, almost enjoying this cat-and-mouse hunt through the box canyon. For reasons Slocum didn't care to examine too closely, he had come alive. Gone was all trace of the pain he'd experienced from the head wound. Every nerve in his lean, hard body tingled as he pitted his wits against the captain's.

"Soon, old girl, soon now," he told his horse. The sorrel looked back as if accusing him of foul deeds, but the horse kept up a steady, even gait that allowed Slocum the time he needed to get the rope riding at the side free.

He peered up the sheer canyon walls and saw the spot on the rim where he had looked down earlier that day. From there it had been only a twenty-minute ride to where Rachel had waited for him. Slocum slapped the sorrel on the rump and slid from the saddle. The horse, no longer burdened by his weight, picked up gait and galloped off, hooves clattering noisily on the rocks.

All this worked to Slocum's benefit. Without a backward look, Slocum started up the rocky slopes. Within minutes, he swam in his own sweat. The work of climbing proved much harder than Slocum had anticipated, but he didn't dare slow now. If a trooper saw him and claimed the dollar bounty, he was a goner. They could form neat lines and fire volley after volley at him until one of them hit him.

But Slocum got his reprieve. Captain O'Malley ordered his troopers after the riderless sorrel, mistaking the sudden burst of speed for fear on Slocum's part. That gave Slocum an extra twenty minutes of climbing. He had almost reached the rim when the shout from below told him he'd been spotted.

Slocum turned and examined the uneven slopes. It took only a few minutes for him to find the rocks he wanted, not for protection but for an offensive weapon. The Apaches had wiped out cavalry patrol after patrol with this trick in Dog Canyon north of El Paso. Cochise had lured more than one patrol into Canyon de Chelly not a hundred miles away, too. Slocum figured it would work just as well for him.

He began prying up large rocks, then releasing them down the slopes. Before they'd gone a dozen yards, a miniature avalanche had formed. A hundred yards later the few rocks had turned into a solid, all-destroying wall of rock. Slocum took no pleasure in the confusion and fear he created in the militia ranks. They were only troopers under orders, as he had been during the War.

But he had a mission to perform, also, and they'd gotten in his way. Fighting the last few feet to the rim, he got his bearings, worked out his best route, and started back to Rachel on foot.

12

Slocum arrived at the tiny camp footsore and tired, but he smiled when he saw Rachel. His tiredness evaporated when she rushed to his arms and kissed him soundly.

"Oh, John, I thought you weren't coming back!"

"Told you I was. But we've got to break camp and get moving. A squad of New Mexico militia decided they wanted me put behind bars in Vermejo." He quickly told the lovely woman all that had happened. "So," he finished, "we've got a few hours head start on them. By the time they figure out how to get out of the box canyon and get on the trail, we've got to be long gone."

"But New Mexico militia? I don't understand. What are they doing in Colorado?"

"Seems their orders are to keep the peace in the San Juan. This General Frost has interpreted it to mean peace anywhere along the San Juan River. Unless I miss my guess by a country mile, what Lew Wallace really meant was for the militia to go after Ike Stockton, no matter where the son of a bitch is."

"We can't run from them all," protested Rachel. "There's too many of them!"

"No choice. We either sit and wait for the militia—or Stockton—or we ride for Durango." Slocum still didn't tell her about the Utes. By now, he hoped, the raiding party had moved on north. Ouray might prove a better place to find horses, or Telluride or Silverton.

"We only have three horses," she said. "The one I rode and the two extra ones."

"We can switch off," he said, becoming irritated. He wanted to ride, not talk. "Get saddled, *now!*"

Rachel's eyes welled with tears, but she didn't actually cry. Slocum went about the chore of making certain the campfire had been properly extinguished, then made a minor effort to hide their presence. He wasn't too successful, but it looked good enough to confuse the troopers for a few minutes. Slocum didn't figure on more than that. Captain O'Malley hadn't struck him as a stupid man, just an overly dedicated one. Sometimes it didn't pay to cleave too closely to a superior's orders.

He'd learned that during the War. And sometimes it had kept him alive.

They rode directly for Durango, throwing caution to the winds. Slocum switched off to the spare horse every hour, Rachel took his, and the one she had been on got a rest. They made good time, but Slocum's sense of time running out chewed at his guts. The only good things about this wild ride were Rachel's lovely figure ahead of him on the trail and the diminishing throb of his head wound. The bullet hadn't cut much more than a shallow groove. With several cleansings from clear mountain streams and Rachel's tender attentions, he decided the wound would heal clean and not give him any trouble.

"What's that?" Rachel called to him. Slocum stopped, leaned forward in the stirrups, and listened intently. A cold-

ness settled in his gut when he decided that the sounds came
from behind along the trail they rode. Hooves. Coming hard.

"Off the trail," he ordered. "Find cover. Up there. In the
pines. Try to keep from kicking up too much of a fuss getting
there." As soon as Rachel had the horses hidden behind a
low rise, Slocum took up fallen limbs still redolent with
pine needles and began brushing away their tracks. He went
back almost a hundred yards along the trail obliterating
hoofmarks, then worked back uphill to the tiny grove of
trees. Tossing the pine brush aside, Slocum dived for cover.

Thundering hooves echoed along the valley. In less than
a minute a dozen men rode by. Slocum peered out and
recognized one or two of them as Stockton's men. Ike Stockton himself brought up the rear. Slocum drew his Colt and
estimated distance and the chance of making a clean shot.

The Colt returned to the cross-draw holster. Stockton
rode like the wind and vanished from sight around a bend
before Slocum knew it. No one in the party slowed enough
to study the trail. Slocum decided they were safe.

For the moment.

"Where were they going in such a hurry?" asked Rachel.

"Where else? Durango." Slocum heaved a sigh and shook
his head. "We got to get back to warn Mrs. Romney that
Stockton knows his men failed. Stockton will be out for
blood this time."

"He was before," Rachel said. She got a far-off look in
her eye, then shuddered. Slocum put his arms around her
and held the woman until she relaxed, buried her face in
his shoulder, and sobbed out the memories tormenting her.

"I'm all right, John." Rachel pushed away, leaving only
a damp spot on his shoulder where her tears had soaked his
shirt. "We must get to Durango and let Mrs. Romney know
we're still alive. She'll see Stockton and think he's done us
in."

Slocum agreed. With Stockton's men riding so hard,

there was no way to reach Durango before them. The best Slocum could hope for was not to arrive too far behind them and give the *Durango Record* owner all the help possible.

The remainder of the day passed in a haze for Slocum. Rachel said little and when she did, it made no sense. She slipped in and out of calling him Luke, and once he thought she addressed him as Mase or Mason. When he asked, Rachel shook her head, as if she had no idea what he wanted from her.

Slocum gave up after this and drifted along, almost sleeping but never quite resting. At sundown he called a halt and scouted for a good place to camp for the night.

"We ought to push on," Rachel insisted. "Stockton's going to be in Durango by now. Mrs. Romney needs us."

"Sheriff Watson might be back by now. And the townspeople were getting a mite upset over Ike coming and shooting up their city, then hightailing it back to his ranch. The Farmington vigilantes aren't much welcome there, either. I think Durango is turning into a force opposing both the vigilantes and Stockton."

"I hope you're right, but what if you're not?" the woman pressed. She stamped her foot and crossed her arms. "Mrs. Romney will need us, no matter how many in town agree with her. The *Record* is all she has. You said Stockton tried to burn her out. What if he does it again? Losing the newspaper would kill her!"

"She's a tough old bird," he said. "It wouldn't set well with her, but she'd go on. Probably build a better print shop. Think of the material it would give her for new editorials." Slocum's attempts to cheer up Rachel didn't work. She huddled down, arms tightly wrapped around herself. Under different, more normal circumstances, Slocum would have let her sulk. She looked too miserable for him to do that now.

"Everything's going to be all right," he soothed. "We'll be able to get back to Durango and help Mrs. Romney. But I don't think she's in any danger."

"You probably said that before Stockton's men kidnapped me." Slocum put his arm around the woman. She turned in toward him, face buried in his chest.

"This kind of range war can't last long. Not with everybody at everyone else's throat. A break's got to come and when it does, Ike Stockton is the one who'll suffer."

"Ike?" she scoffed. "I doubt it. He's got Clay Allison on his side. You know the kind of man he is."

Slocum had heard Allison's name again and again, but nothing indicated Clay Allison was within five hundred miles of San Juan County. He started to tell Rachel that one man didn't make a fight successful, then stopped. She didn't want to hear that. She wanted comforting of a more physical nature.

Of a more intimate kind.

Her face, damp with tears, lifted. Their eyes met. Slocum studied every line of her finely boned face, the high cheeks, the lovely blue eyes, the straight nose, the slightly pouting lips. He kissed her. They sank back to the pine-needle-covered ground and crushed the fragrant carpet with their bodies.

"Oh, John, I need you so!" she moaned out. Her lips hungrily devoured his, her kisses turning more and more fervent. Fingers raking at his back, the woman conveyed her need to him.

"Are you sure?" he asked, breaking away for a moment to look down at Rachel. "It's not been that long since..."

"Help me forget them. Help me, John, help me!"

She pulled him back for another long, passionate kiss. While Slocum had some misgivings, he decided this might be what the woman really needed. There wasn't any doubt in his mind she *wanted* him. Slocum finally decided it might be like riding a horse. Get thrown, get back on.

All thoughts except about the growing urgency in his loins vanished. He kissed her full lips, then moved his mouth back along the line of her jaw until he found the shell-like ear. He nibbled. She gasped and pressed herself harder against him, silently demanding more. His tongue darted out and made a wet, teasing circuit, duplicating what would be happening lower on their bodies.

"Too slow, John, you're going too slow. Do it now. Do it now!"

He kept on at his own pace. Even though he wanted to give in to Rachel's suggestion, he felt he owed it to her after all that had happened to prove that making love was different from rape. He never wanted her to think of that awful occurrence again, not if she could think of better experiences, pleasant times with him.

He kissed her slender throat, felt her response, then moved even lower. His fingers worked at the flannel shirt she wore. The too-large garment gaped open to expose twin mounds of creamy flesh that tempted Slocum too much to move on. First one trembling breast and then the other received his full attention. His tongue looped and toyed with the rubbery button cresting her left breast, then he slowly licked over to give the right nipple the same treatment. Beneath his tongue those coral buds blossomed and hardened.

He worked even lower.

Rachel gasped and moaned incoherently now. Her slender fingers laced through his thick black hair and guided him in the direction they both wanted.

He unfastened the belt and pulled down the trousers the woman wore. The dark brown triangle of fur between her legs was already dotted with droplets showing her arousal. Thick fingers explored the tangled mat between her well-fleshed thighs, then dipped into her most intimate recesses.

"Oh, oh!" she gasped out. "My pussy's on fire. Fuck me, Luke, fuck me good!"

Slocum sat upright, staring at her. His hardness began to go away. Rachel calling him by her dead lover's name took the thrill out of any lovemaking.

Rachel seemed not to know whose name she'd called out. She looked up at Slocum with nothing but lust in her gaze. If he wanted to stop, she wanted nothing more than to continue.

"Your turn," she said, licking her lips.

"No, wait," Slocum said, but the woman's fingers stripped off his vest and shirt and tugged at his balky gunbelt. Slocum relented and let her get the gunbelt free and start pulling down his trousers. When the cool evening air blew across his groin, he had deflated to half the size he'd been.

Rachel didn't allow that condition to continue. Her eager lips closed on the tip of his manhood. Slocum grunted as her mouth worked on him, restoring the cock to workable length.

"I want you," she said in a voice almost too low to be heard. In the gathering darkness he peered down at her. Rachel's eyes took on an animal glow in the twilight. Her tongue licked over her lips again, beckoning him on. The scent of crushed pine needles mingled with the musk of her arousal. The coral tips of her breasts pulsed visibly every time her heart beat.

Slocum pushed her onto her back, moved between her wantonly opened legs with his body, and said, "Guide me in. I like the feel of your hand on me."

She smiled wickedly. He gasped again as slender fingers closed around his turgid manhood and tugged him forward with a boldness he appreciated. The first brush told how wet she was. He moved slower now, entering her heated interior one slow inch at a time. The delightful torture caused them both to gasp with joy.

Then neither could hold back. Animal passions unleashed, they bucked and rolled, straining as one. When Slocum spilled his seed into her depths, Rachel arched her back and let out a howl that rivaled any mating coyote's. Her fingers clawed at his back and then she sank down to the ground, pinned by his weight.

"You are so good," she sighed. She kissed his ear.

He lifted himself up and stared at her. Should he tell her how she'd called him "Luke," or should he let it ride? Rachel Burnham had been through so much. Who was he to say what thoughts rose within her mind at unguarded moments? And Crazy Matt had said he looked like Rachel's dead lover.

It rankled, though. Slocum wanted the woman to want him, not the memory of this Luke.

"We'd better be getting on. Sun's already down. We've been riding all day and it'll be damn near midnight before we reach Durango."

"I'm hungry, John. Can't we wait just a little longer?"

"I reckon so." He started to push himself off her, but insistent hands held him between her spread legs.

"I'm hungry," Rachel said, "but not for food. For you!" The kiss left nothing to the imagination. Slocum decided he was getting hungry again, too.

"Utes!" Rachel cried. "You were worried about Indians and you didn't tell me?" She spun in the saddle and glared at him. "Did you think I'd faint? After all I've been through the past few days?"

"Didn't want to add to your concern," he said. They had ridden steadily for six hours since their interlude beneath the pines. Traces of Stockton's passage were everywhere, but so were signs of a Ute raiding party. Slocum guessed it was the main body and numbered at least fifteen braves. He'd been damned lucky not to run into it instead of the smaller band.

"I'm no expert woodsman," she said, "but I can tell the signs. And Sheriff Watson had said this was where they were doing most of their mischief."

"I'm more worried about the New Mexico militia," Slocum said. "If that captain in command of the column has any sense, he'd have overtaken us already. Is there another route to Durango he might have followed?"

"These mountains are filled with tiny notches and passes for men willing to take chances. It's only when you get further north into the Rockies that passes across the higher reaches are hard to come by. This captain might have gone along the Denver & Rio Grande tracks."

Slocum nodded. That had been the route he'd wanted to take to avoid the Utes.

"If he rides hard, he might arrive in Durango before we do." Slocum closed his eyes and tried to imagine the carnage that a collision between Captain O'Malley and Ike Stockton would cause. Durango might not be left standing.

"Do you think Mrs. Romney is all right?" Rachel bit her lower lip. "And Billy. He was supposed to be out doing chores for Mrs. Romney. Riding around, asking what people thought. He was all excited by the notion of being a real reporter."

"He's a smart boy. He'll stay out of trouble." But Slocum knew that just being smart wouldn't keep Billy or anyone else out of trouble. The entire San Juan Basin had caught fire. Anyone riding through it could get their fingers burned and never know why.

"John, listen! Gunshots!"

"How far are we from Durango?"

"Not more than two miles. We round a bend and get by

142   Jake Logan

the hill to the east of town and we can look down on it."

Slocum said nothing more. He used his reins to whip his
tired horse into a trot. Anything more and the animal might
have collapsed from exhaustion beneath him. Only when
they arrived at the vantage point promised by Rachel did
he pull back and stare.

"Looks like the Fourth of July," Slocum said. "The entire
town's caught up in a fight!"

"Maybe not," Rachel said. "I'd forgot."

"Forgot what?" he demanded.

"In all the . . . excitement." She patted her tangled hair
into a semblance of order. "The West End Hotel's finished
up its construction. They'd scheduled a gala opening 'round
about now. Mrs. Romney had mentioned firecrackers and
free beer. Some of the women didn't much cotton to that
idea, but with Ike Stockton and the Farmington posse riding
back and forth, they finally agreed the townspeople needed
something to let off steam."

"That's nothing more than a hotel opening?" Slocum
asked. He frowned and stared down at Durango. The rapid-
fire reports might be from firecrackers, but they didn't come
in the familiar patterns.

"I'm sure that's all it is," Rachel said.

"I'm not. See there? That's a fire burning out of control.
And remember, Stockton beat us to Durango. Think he'd
join in drinking beer and setting off firecrackers?"

"He tried to kidnap Mrs. Romney," Rachel said in a small
voice.

"The militia's had time to arrive, too. Captain O'Malley
might have taken it into his head to take Stockton back to
New Mexico. Anything to keep the peace along the San
Juan," Slocum finished sarcastically.

The loud reports from Durango sounded less and less
like firecrackers and more and more like gunshots.

"Stay here," Slocum said. "I'll go see what's happening."

"No!"

He glared at her, then saw the firm set to her chin. He'd have to hogtie Rachel to keep her from riding down there with him.

"Stay close," he said, giving in. "And don't get that pretty head of yours shot off."

Together, they rode down into the middle of a full-scale battle.

13

"Around behind the *Record*," Slocum shouted to Rachel Burnham. "There's not as much action there."

Slocum saw the auburn head nod. Other than this, he had no idea if she even heard him. From all sides came gunfire. Slocum hardly believed his eyes as they raced along the outskirts of Durango. Some buildings had been turned into structures that might have been built from worm-rotted wood. Holes large enough to poke his fist through showed the insides of those buildings, and in some places, the walls had begun crumbling. He had seen destruction worse than this, but it had been during the War and had been caused by entire armies.

Riding through the Shenandoah Valley had been grim. Slocum had seen entire farms blown to hell and gone by artillery fire. But that had been heavy cannon and Minie balls doing the damage. Here it was accomplished by hundreds—thousands—of rounds hitting the buildings.

The soldier in Slocum wondered how so much ammunition had been carried by Stockton and his men.

A hail of bullets drove him forward over the neck of his horse. The animal snorted in fear, eyes showing white around the brown. It took all Slocum's considerable skill to keep the horse from bolting and running wild. When he fought it to a halt, he'd arrived behind Mrs. Romney's newspaper building.

The *Record* had escaped—at least, it hadn't been destroyed by hundreds upon hundreds of bullets ripping it apart. Slocum saw a few black holes in the wood siding, mostly lit from inside by a flickering pale yellow flame.

"The building's on fire!" cried Rachel.

"Don't think so," Slocum answered. "Stay down and let me go check." When Rachel tried to join him, he took her firmly by the arms and shoved her against the building. "Stay here," he repeated. "I don't want Mrs. Romney putting a bullet in you, thinking it was Ike Stockton."

He saw her nod reluctantly. He spun, dropped into a crouch, and made his way to the largest hole. It had to be a .45, from the size of the cavity left in the wall. Slocum put his eye to the hole and peered into the print shop.

As he'd guessed, the *Durango Record* wasn't on fire. Mrs. Romney was walking around holding a coal-oil lamp above her head. In her other hand she carried the rusty ball and powder Remington that Rachel had used on Stockton's men earlier. From the set of the woman's shoulders and the way she held her head high, Slocum guessed anyone trying to break into the newspaper would get a hot reception.

He returned to Rachel and told her, "I'm going in. Wait for me to call out that it's all right to enter."

Slocum cut off any discussion and returned to the side of the building. From there he cautiously made his way to the front. The gunfire had died down a mite. He didn't see how it could keep up that deadly level for long. Rifle barrels would start melting down if they didn't give their weapons a rest.

He crawled on his belly to the door. The boards he had nailed over the windows were mostly filled with holes. Slocum pounded on the door and got a heavy slug as response.

"You just get the hell out of Durango, Ike Stockton!" shouted Mrs. Romney. The sound of the pistol cocking rumbled like springtime thunder over the Rockies. "You try kidnapping me again and I'll blow your balls off!"

"Mrs. Romney!" Slocum shouted. "It's me. I got Rachel with me. You and Billy all right?"

"John? That you, John Slocum?"

"Yes!"

"Well, why didn't you say so? Letting me shoot at you like that. Damnation!" Mrs. Romney got the door open. From the scraping sounds inside, Slocum figured she had something heavy blocking the door. Slocum dived through the crack she opened for him. He rolled and came up, back against the front counter.

"You surely do make an entrance, John," Mrs. Romney observed. "But then, these are dramatic times, aren't they?"

"What's going on? The town's turning to wormwood from all the gunfire."

"Ruined the West End Hotel opening," she said. "The whole town had been looking forward to it for weeks. Biggest event in months. Stockton and his men came riding in, shooting and carrying on. Poor old Mr. Cramer at the First National Bank thought it was a holdup. He got out his shotgun and started shooting."

"And Stockton's men shot back," said Slocum.

"That's what happened. By the time anyone sorted out what was really going on, everyone was out in the street shooting at everyone else. Sheriff Watson lost control early on. Can't blame him for wanting to stay clear."

"I can't either," said Slocum. "How long's the battle been raging?" He still couldn't believe the intensity of the fighting. By peering out between a crack formed by board and window frame, he got a good view of the West End Hotel.

The grand opening wouldn't be possible for at least two weeks, maybe longer. The damage looked extensive enough to keep carpenters hard at work just to fix up the damage to the front. Of the interior and the damage to its fixtures, Slocum didn't even want to guess.

He craned around and tried to get some idea of what went on down Railroad Street where the saloons stood. The constant flare of pistols and rifles firing told him that was an unhealthy part of town. Both the locals and Stockton's men had broken into the saloons and gotten liquored up. They might not hit what they aimed at, but the flying lead made life chancy out on the streets.

"They been going at it like that for well nigh four hours," Mrs. Romney said. "Stockton didn't expect organized resistance when he came whoopin' and a-hollerin' into town."

"What organized resistance?" Slocum asked. "The New Mexico militia?"

"Whatever gave you that notion? That's the newly established Durango Committee of Safety holding forth against Stockton."

Slocum looked at the newspaper editor, silently waiting for the explanation. It wasn't long in coming.

"One of my editorials finally roused them," Mrs. Romney said with fire in her voice. "This morning I got it out on the streets. Didn't let a blessed one of them get by me without at least looking at it, and most bought a copy. I told them about Rachel's kidnapping, how Ike had tried to burn down the *Record*—everything I could, I threw into that piece. Damned good work, even if I do say so myself."

"So the good citizens of Durango went and formed a vigilante committee, just like the one in Farmington."

"Nothing wrong with defending yourself. We had enough of Stockton. It was about time they did something."

"It gets lonely being the only voice crying out in the wilderness," Slocum said. Mrs. Romney started to comment on his sarcasm when he spoke up, drowning her out. "I got to get Rachel in. She's waiting for me out back."

"Don't!" cried Mrs. Romney when Slocum headed for the door leading into the back room. "I booby-trapped that way. You'll have to go back out the front."

"Why'd you do that?"

"Couldn't look after both front and back by myself. I sent Billy off to get him out of the line of fire. Didn't think he'd be much safer, but considering what Ike tried before, I rested easier with Billy over at the sheriff's office. Told him he was our man on the scene and to get as much for a feature as he could." Mrs. Romney chuckled and shook her graying head. "I do declare, he might have the stuff of a reporter in him. Took to it like a duck takes to water."

"Don't plug us when we get back," Slocum said. He slid back onto the wood sidewalk in front of the *Record,* around the side, and eventually to the back. Rachel waited impatiently for him there.

"You certainly took your sweet time of it!" she raged. "Leaving me out here like that!"

He silenced her with a kiss. Flustered, Rachel backed off, not sure what to do or say.

"Now that we have that out of the way," he said, "follow me into the print shop. There's nobody shooting at the *Record* right now, so we ought not have any problems."

Rachel nodded mutely and obeyed. Slocum dropped down to retrace his path, but he had misjudged the ebb and flow of battle in Durango. A large splinter leaped off the sidewalk in front of his face as a bullet gouged its way to a stop in the wall.

"Get inside!" he shouted to Rachel. He pushed the woman past him while he rolled and crouched behind a watering trough, Colt drawn and ready.

The orange muzzle flash from the rifle caught his attention. Someone had climbed to the roof of the demolished West End Hotel and commanded much of the street. Slocum waited, saw the orange tongue lash forth again, then carefully fired. His first shot went to the left of the muzzle flash, the next to the right, the third between. He repeated the bracketing pattern and received a reward on the fifth shot when a man shrieked in pain. Slocum saw a carbine fall over the edge of the roof. When it landed in the street, it discharged, adding still another piece of lead to the rain of death.

Of the rifleman, Slocum heard nothing more.

He smiled. A .31 Colt Navy at this distance against a rifle—and he'd won. Experience and skill against armament. He felt damn good about the shot.

Slocum sobered when he realized just how good he did feel. He had come alive. The smell of gunpowder in the air didn't choke him, it revitalized him. Every nerve in his body sang as he pitted himself against everyone else in Durango.

The desolation he experienced in that instant wiped away any thrill. It made him a little sick when he realized that he *needed* this carnage. Anything less struck him as dull and unworthy of his time.

He *needed* being in the middle of the death and destruction. This was the legacy of the War and riding with Quantrill and Bloody Bill Anderson and Cole Younger and all the other Redlegs.

Slocum ducked back into the *Record* office and closed the door. Mrs. Romney moved the small letter press back across the door, preventing anyone from breaking in without making a monumental ruckus.

"Go on and reload. I'll keep a lookout," said Mrs. Romney.

Slocum started to say what ammunition he needed was with the rest of his belongings in the back room when Mrs. Romney pointed. She had brought his meager possessions into the main office before booby-trapping the back door.

"Thought it might be of use," the newspaper editor said. "But couldn't get it to work in this." She hefted the black powder Remington. "Good thing I haven't had to use this old cannon. Not sure I could be as good as Rachel."

The look that went between the two women puzzled Slocum. Mrs. Romney appeared accusing; Rachel seemed to take no notice, as if she didn't understand.

The uneasy spell shattered when half a dozen rifle bullets ripped away at the boards over the windows. Slocum got both women down behind the huge cast-iron printing press. Only once did a bullet hit the press, ricocheting around the *Record* print shop.

"It might be a long night," Slocum said, settling down.

Mrs. Romney set the coal-oil lamp on the floor and turned it down to a dull yellow glow. "Reckon you're right, John. Might as well make the most of it." She pulled paper and pen and ink down from her desktop and began writing.

Mrs. Romney looked up, smiled, and said, "Tomorrow's editorial about how bad Durango looks. Going to do a sidebar on reopening the West End Hotel." She scribbled for a few minutes, then added, "Hope Billy's got some good coverage from the sheriff's office."

"I do, too," Slocum said. Rachel curled up next to him, head against his shoulder. In seconds she slept peacefully, in spite of the sporadic gunfire outside. Mrs. Romney wrote and Slocum stared off into the dark corners of the shop, lost in his own thoughts.

"Hard to believe," Mrs. Romney said. "Circulation's up almost twenty percent. Can't say as I like the idea of Ike Stockton shooting up the town just to sell papers, but some good has come from him."

"It's been over a week," Rachel said happily, "and people are still buying the *Record* to find out what Stockton's up to."

Slocum looked up from his repair work when Sheriff Watson walked in, tipped his hat, and said, "Stockton's still creating news, I'm afraid. Me and Sullivan are off to Silverton."

"Why? What's happened?" Slocum climbed down from the ladder and dropped the paintbrush into the whitewash he used on the ceiling. Since the entire office had been so badly shot up, he had decided to renovate from top to bottom.

"Hard to tell, since the telegraph between here'n Silverton is out. Damned Utes." Sheriff Watson spat accurately and hit a spittoon at the corner of the counter.

"Must be important to get both you and Deputy Sullivan out of town," Slocum said.

A grim expression settled on Sheriff Watson's face. "Word's come in that three of Stockton's boys went treasure hunting. Tried to find some booty left by Kid Thomas' brother when he got sent up for robbing the Fort Lewis payroll."

"Who got killed?" Slocum took a wild shot at what had happened. Only something of real importance would roust Sheriff Watson from Durango after the town got shot up.

"Burt Wilkinson, Dyson Eskridge and Kid Thomas ran afoul Marshal Ogsbury."

"The law in Silverton?" asked Slocum.

"The former marshal. They were drunk, they had the payroll money, and they got spooked. One of them killed him."

"So you're going after them?"

"Don't go sticking your nose where it don't belong, Slocum," came Sullivan's cold voice. "This don't concern you none. Sheriff, I got the horses ready. Over at the stable, when you're finished here."

"Thanks," Sheriff Watson said. He watched Sullivan turn and stalk off angrily.

"What's got him so riled?" asked Mrs. Romney

"Not what; who. Ike Stockton did something nobody thought he'd do. He tracked down his own men and turned them over to a lynch mob. The mob hanged Kid Thomas outright. Figured any nigger deserved it, just on general principles." Sheriff Watson spat again, his face set into hard lines. Slocum realized the man wanted every single man in that lynch mob brought up on murder charges, but it would never happen.

"And," Sheriff Watson went on, after wiping his mouth on his sleeve, "they strung up Eskridge next. Burt's still lingering in the jail whilst they argue over his fate. Can't seem to decide if he did anything or not. I figure he's already been strung up, though. The mob had that look about them."

Watson spat again. "Burt Wilkerson and Sullivan there are closer'n most brothers. Don't think my deputy's going to stop until he gets Ike."

"You mean Stockton turned over his own men to a lynch mob?" Mrs. Romney stared in disbelief.

"Worse'n that. He did it for money. Silverton had put up a reward. Ogsbury was a right popular man."

Even Slocum failed to understand Stockton's motives. All he knew of the man came at second hand, but Stockton hadn't seemed treacherous to his own. Granted, killing a town marshal was bad, but if those three owlhoots *were* his men, Stockton owed them more loyalty than he'd shown. To turn over his own ranch hands for the reward, then stand by and watch two of them be hanged and let the third languish in jail seemed beyond even Ike Stockton's lowdown ways.

"Sullivan wants Stockton bad. Can't say I blame him. Sentiment in Durango's blowing that way, too. And I'm not fighting it much. Well, Mrs. Romney, be seeing you in a week or less, if God's willin' and the creek don't rise." Sheriff Watson tipped his hat again and left, walking briskly in the direction of the stables.

"Rachel!" shouted Mrs. Romney, getting the girl out of the back room. "Pull the lead story. We got a new one for an extra." Mrs. Romney rubbed her ink-stained hands together in glee. "This is just like the big-time papers in San Francisco and Chicago. Durango's going to have an extra edition on the streets before sundown."

She hurried to her desk and began writing up the story. Rachel set to getting the letterpress ready for the new page while Billy Burnham got to work toting supplies from the back. Slocum just watched. This wasn't his job. He picked up the bucket of whitewash and stepped out onto the sidewalk.

Everywhere he looked, Durango bustled with activity. The people were working hard to rebuild their city. But with the industry had come a change Slocum had noted over the past week. Before, Ike Stockton could do no wrong. Whatever he wanted, the people of Durango backed.

Ever since the incident on the night of the West End Hotel opening, sentiment had been turning against the cattleman. Nobody openly sided with the sodbusters or the Farmington vigilantes or the Santa Fe Ring and their attempt to steal the Maxwell Land Grant and Railway Company, but their support of Stockton had diminished.

Word that Stockton had turned in his own men for a paltry reward would turn every hand against the man in Durango.

Slocum didn't find himself feeling the least bit sorry for the man.

With any luck, the San Juan War would be over soon. He leaned against the railing in front of the *Record* and wondered how many of these good people would be dead before it became history. He didn't think much of their Committee of Safety—or the Farmington vigilantes. Slocum had had his brushes with the law in the past, but he always preferred seeing justice resting in just one set of hands.

The hands might be bloodstained, they might be honest, but no matter, they were always better than a mob bent on nothing but mindless vengeance and seeing some poor bastard strung up.

Slocum touched his neck and shuddered at the memory of the coarse hemp noose.

Slocum turned back to the sound of the letterpress beginning its slow, messy work of informing all Durango. Rachel and Mrs. Romney might need a strong back now. Running that press required more strength than determination after the first few pages came off. He went inside and got busy.

14

"Can't rightly say," Mrs. Romney told Slocum. "Why do you ask a thing like that?"

Slocum shrugged. "I was just curious. Since you took Billy and Rachel in like you did, I thought you knew something more about her parents."

"You're talking about Billy and Rachel, but then you turn around and say '*her*' parents. It's Rachel you're interested in, isn't it, John?"

"Won't pretend otherwise."

"She's had some hard times," Mrs. Romney said. "She won't speak of her folks, even to me. And Billy was too young to really remember. It's been a while."

"Didn't even know that," Slocum said. He frowned. He kept getting contradictory impressions from Billy and Rachel. The boy said one thing, his sister another. So much of the way Rachel acted surprised him. She still confused him and

Luke at moments of extreme passion. Slocum didn't like that one bit, but he found it almost impossible to speak of it to Rachel. She seemed not to notice at all.

"If you want to know anything about Luke, you'll have to ask her. Damned shame about him. Damned shame."

"Accidents happen," Slocum said.

"Accident? What are you talking about?"

"Rachel said he was kicked in the head by his horse and died."

Slocum's face melted into an expressionless mask when he saw Mrs. Romney's reaction. Her eyes widened and her mouth opened and closed like a fish out of water. "It wasn't like that at all. Luke upped and left. One day he was here, the next he was nowhere to be seen. The best anyone could figure, he walked out on Rachel."

"Did Luke have any friends who might know?"

"Luke was something of a loner. Never saw him with anyone before Rachel. No friends I heard of." Mrs. Romney ran an inky hand through her gray hair, not noticing or caring about the stain it left. "He was a lot like you in many ways."

"Crazy Matt told me Luke looked like me." At the thought of the old man, Slocum reached into his pocket and felt the two pecans. Those were all Matt possessed when he got gunned down. He took them out, stared at them, and finally tucked them back into his pants pocket. He'd get around to eating them one day.

"Looked a lot like you, John." Mrs. Romney turned when Deputy Johnson sauntered into the *Record* office. "What can I do for you, Charlie? Got a scoop for the afternoon edition?"

"Nothing of the sort, Mrs. Romney. Things been quiet. I like it like that," he said. "Sheriff Watson told me before him and Sullivan went off to Silverton to look in on you now and again. Any troubles?" Johnson stared straight at Slocum.

"No troubles to speak of, not at the moment. You can rest easy on that score. *I'd* rest a mite easier if you'd lock up that scalawag Ike Stockton."

"That's what Sheriff Watson's trying to do up in Silverton. Don't think Sullivan'd let the son of a bitch live to stand trial, though. He and Burt Wilkinson were close, damned close."

"And Sheriff Watson had a real liking for Ogsbury, too. Well, Ike can't go on like he's been doing, turning on his friends."

"Why do you think he turned his men over to the mob?" asked Slocum. He lounged back against the counter.

"Because he's a snake in the grass, that's why," Charlie Johnson answered. "Don't need no other reason than that. Just goes to show you shouldn't go cozying up to his kind."

"You from back East?"

"Iowa," Johnson said. "What's it to you?"

Slocum shrugged. Charlie Johnson came from sodbuster country. Since Slocum had heard Stockton came from down Cleburne, Texas way, that'd be another bone of contention between the men, as if they needed it. Stockton was a cattleman, the lawman was from a farm background. And Johnson had to think constantly of having the Farmington vigilantes take him out and try to string him up because Johnson was Stockton's "man."

"When the people read *this* editorial, there won't be any sympathy left for Ike Stockton," the woman said. She slammed her fist down on the counter, startling Johnson. Slocum said nothing, watching the two. "You want to give it a once-over, Charlie, before it hits the street?" She pulled a freshly printed page off the press and gingerly passed it to Johnson.

"Got work to do, Mrs. Romney. Thanks. Read it later."
Johnson slipped away and almost ran from the shop.

"Can't read, can he?" Slocum asked.

"Doubt it. If he can, he doesn't do too good a job at it.
Sheriff Watson didn't hire him for his brains. But don't get
me wrong. Charlie Johnson is a good man. If nothing out
of the ordinary happens."

"Hasn't been too much use lately, then," Slocum observed.

Mrs. Romney nodded. "Not much," she agreed. "Don't
just stand there. Get those papers in the box. Billy's getting
ready to take them down to the corner of Railroad and Main
to sell them. Can't keep the *Record*'s readers waiting for
the news."

Slocum dropped stack after stack of the freshly printed
Record into a wooden crate and hefted it. He guessed Mrs.
Romney ran twice the pages as she had before. The range
war had sparked interest, and everyone in Durango wanted
to read about all the details—those who weren't out par-
ticipating in the gunplay. Durango's Committee of Safety
still patrolled the street, even though Stockton was supposed
to be somewhere to the north around Silverton. Slocum
didn't like the looks of the Committee of Safety. Vigilantes
were vigilantes, no matter what they called themselves.

But he had to admit their continual presence had a calm-
ing effect on many others in the town, Charlie Johnson
included.

"Get those out to Billy, will you?" Mrs. Romney shouted
from the rear of the shop. "And tell that good-for-nothing
not to come back until everyone in Durango has a copy!"

Slocum laughed and shifted the box to his shoulder. He
turned outside and went toward the corner, where the boy
had already whipped up interest in the edition.

". . . hot off the presses!" Billy yelled. "Here they come.

Don't crowd, don't crowd. Get your *Record!*"

Slocum dropped the box and helped Billy with the initial
crush of people. Many turned directly to Mrs. Romney's
editorial blast against Ike Stockton and walked away reading
it and muttering to themselves. Slocum hadn't seen the
proofs on the editorial, but he knew Mrs. Romney was
especially pleased with it. He wondered if she shouldn't
have printed the newspaper on asbestos, from the reaction
he observed.

"Gosh, Mr. Slocum, this is the best we done—ever!"

In less than fifteen minutes, Billy had only a dozen papers
left out of almost a hundred.

"Just goes to show," Slocum said. "No matter what the
trouble, somebody's going to profit. Without Ike Stockton,
Mrs. Romney wouldn't have been able to get a readership
as big as she has in the past week or two."

"Never thought of it that way," Billy said.

Slocum started to ask the boy where his sister was when
the thunder of horses filled Durango's main street. Slocum
heaved a mighty sigh and turned to see who it was this time
that invaded the city. It might sell another hundred copies
of the *Record*'s next edition, but Slocum wished that whoever
was riding in had just bypassed the town entirely. He was
tired of ducking wild shots.

"Damn!" Billy cried. "It's Ike! He's come back to Durango to kill us all!"

Slocum grabbed the boy by the collar and kept him from
running. He spun the boy around and dropped him just inside
the door of Larkin's Dry Goods Store. "Stay here," Slocum
ordered. "You won't be in the line of fire if trouble starts.
And it may not. Looks like Stockton is heading for the
sheriff's office. Wait a few minutes, then hightail it back
to the *Record*."

"Mr. Slocum, no!" the teenager protested. "There's a

story brewing there. I want to get it!"

Slocum sighed. Mrs. Romney had done too good a job instilling devotion to the story in the boy. No matter what the personal risk, the press had to be fed a continual source of information.

"Stay here." The bark in his voice caused Billy to back away, eyes wide.

Slocum walked along the sidewalk. Already members of the Committee of Safety formed in tight knots, whispering among themselves. Slocum didn't wait to see what they'd do. Whatever it was, he wanted no part of it. He crossed the street to the sheriff's office, slipping the leather thong off the hammer of his Colt as he went.

Eight of Stockton's men stood apprehensively outside the sheriff's office. Inside, Slocum heard Stockton's and Johnson's voices. Johnson shouted at the renegade.

As Slocum started into the office, one of Stockton's henchmen reached out to stop him. Slocum turned slightly, took the restraining wrist in a deceptively light grip and twisted hard. The man yelped in pain and dropped to his knees.

"I've got business with the deputy," Slocum said. He released the offending hand and walked in. Deputy Johnson spun at his entry, started to bark out an order to leave, then figured Slocum was on his side.

"Slocum," the deputy said. "What do you want?"

"Just come by to pass the time," he said. Stockton noted the stance, the way Slocum's hand never drifted far from the worn ebony butt of his Colt Navy, and the determination burning in Slocum's green eyes.

"Be with you in a minute," Johnson said, turning back to Stockton. "Mr. Stockton, you're not wanted in Durango. You wore out your welcome with the way you shot up everything at the West End's grand opening. Hell, Stockton, they haven't even got it pieced back together yet, and it's been over a week!"

"We need a day or two to rest up," Stockton said. "We're not asking for anything special. Sheriff Watson'd let us stay if he was here."

"Hell, Mr. Stockton, Sheriff Watson's up in Silverton taking care of a mess *you* created." Deputy Johnson paced nervously, obviously not sure what to do. He glanced over at Slocum, who nodded slightly. Johnson came to his conclusion. "I'm sorry. You'll have to leave town. I don't want you here stirrin' up more trouble."

"You can't do that!" raged Stockton. "We got troubles. They're hot on our heels. All we want is to hole up here for a day or two. When they're gone, we can amble on back to the spread out at Animas."

"Who's this on your trail?" Slocum asked.

"If it's any of your business, mister, and it ain't, we got a bunch of New Mexico bushwhackers after us."

"Bushwhackers or militia?"

"No difference."

"Big difference. These wear uniforms and have orders from Governor Wallace."

"What do you know of this?" asked Johnson. "This is Colorado. The New Mexico militia doesn't have no authority here."

"They've got about twenty rifles' worth of authority," Slocum said. "Deputy Johnson, you want them coming into Durango to pry loose *him?*"

That convinced Johnson.

"We got more'n twenty rifles willin' to get you out of town right now, Mr. Stockton. The Durango Committee of Safety was formed just after you shot up the damned place. We won't let you do it again. You've got ten minutes to get the hell out of Durango!"

"You—" Stockton launched himself across the desk and grabbed Johnson by the throat. Then Stockton screeched in pain as Slocum drew his Colt and brought it smashing down hard into the man's arm. Nerveless, Stockton's arm flopped about. Stockton stepped back, astounded that anyone would touch him. Then he saw that he walked a fine line between life and death. Slocum held himself in check only through great willpower. He remembered that the man had ordered Mrs. Romney kidnapped and the *Record* burned to the ground, and that Stockton's men had raped Rachel.

If Stockton hadn't so many men outside and the potential for a real massacre, Slocum would have taken him then and there.

"You heard the deputy," said Slocum. "Leave town— on your horse or slung over it. Take your pick."

"You're dead men. Both of you. I swear it on my mother's grave. God damn, you're both dead men!"

Stockton stormed from the office. Slocum heard him shout at his men. The clatter of hooves signalled Stockton's retreat. Slocum turned back to Johnson. The deputy sat at the desk, sweating buckets.

"Never thought I could do it," he said. "Look at this. My hands are quaking like aspen leaves. Damnation."

"You're a lawman. You didn't have much choice." Slocum looked out the window and saw twenty or more members of the Durango Committee of Safety across the street. All fingered their rifles and shotguns as if they'd never seen the weapons before in their lives. Slocum saw only trouble if Stockton had stayed. Someone—a hothead or a man too nervous to think straight—would have started a bloodbath if Stockton hadn't left.

"Thanks, Slocum."

"Read about it in the *Record*," Slocum said, leaving. He sucked in a deep breath outside, the sunlight warm on his face. It was turning into a fine spring. Another six weeks or so would bring real summer to the high Rockies. Slocum had seen it before, but never with the intention of staying in one place and letting it surround him.

Slocum stopped and peered up and down the street. Something bothered him and he couldn't figure out what it was. The Committee of Safety had dispersed now that Stockton had gone, but tension remained behind. Slocum began walking toward the *Record* office, then stopped. He spun and looked sharply down a side street toward the stables.

Nothing.

"Getting spooked," he said to himself. He hurried back to the newspaper office, anxious to see Rachel. With Stockton so near, he worried about her. She had shown no ill effects of being raped by Stockton's men, and that worried Slocum more than if she'd shouted or cried or carried on. Rachel had buried the awful experience, and Slocum had the fear that all the venom caused by the rape would come spilling out when it was least expected.

Slocum rounded the street corner just in time to see Rachel leave the office and go rushing off in the opposite direction.

He called after her, but the woman didn't acknowledge that she'd even heard him. Slocum's ire rose at this. There was no way in hell she couldn't have heard him. He went into the *Record* office and saw Mrs. Romney standing behind the counter, tears running down her cheeks.

"What's wrong?" he demanded.

"Rachel. She . . . she heard Stockton was in town. She took my pistol and went after him."

"She's got a long ways to go," Slocum said, relaxing a mite. "Deputy Johnson chased Stockton out of town. Stockton's probably halfway back to Animas City by now."

"No, Mr. Slocum. He's not. I saw Ike over at the stables. He didn't leave at all. I came back here and told Mrs. Romney. And Rachel overheard. I didn't know she was here, honest!"

"Don't worry your head none, Billy," Mrs. Romney soothed. "She'd've found out some other way."

Slocum said nothing to either. He spun and ran from the office, intent on getting to the stables before Rachel. She had taken a longer path, but it would bring her in from a blind side, allowing her to sneak up on anyone inside. Slocum had no desire to surprise Stockton. Quite the contrary. He wanted the man out of town as fast as possible—and away from Rachel Burnham.

Slocum started down the side street leading to the stables and heard rifles cocking ahead of him. From the loft and the double doors in front muzzles poked out aimed in his direction.

"Leave us be, Slocum!" called out Stockton. "We just want to rest and then we're on our way. This ain't your fight. You get on out of here now!"

Slocum couldn't warn Stockton. To do so spelled Rachel's death warrant. About Stockton he cared not one whit. Let her kill him if she could, but Slocum feared the rest of Stockton's men would, in turn, kill Rachel.

Slocum held his hands out, palms up, and backed off. He didn't care what the men inside the stable thought, even though their jeers rang in his ears. All he wanted was to see Rachel away and safe.

He circled, squeezing down littered alleyways and through a burned-out shell of a store. Slocum saw Rachel walking grimly, the heavy Remington in her hands.

"Rachel, wait!" he called out.

She ignored him and kept walking. He judged distances and knew he had misjudged. She'd arrive at the stable doors before he could reach her.

"Stockton!" she called out, her voice shrill and threatening to break with strain. "Get out here!"

"Who's there?" Slocum heard Ike Stockton call.

"Get out here!"

Rachel lifted the heavy gun and fired when one of Stockton's men poked his head out to see who summoned his boss. The pistol bucked hard and staggered Rachel, but she recovered and moved forward again to seek out Stockton and kill him.

Slocum cast caution to the winds and ran all out to get to Rachel. She had killed the man she'd fired at; he sprawled face down in the dirt, half in and half out of the stable. From inside came frantic voices.

Rachel fired again. And again.

"What's going on?" came Stockton's loud cry. "That the bitch from the *Record*? Damnation. Thought she'd been taken care of." Rachel fired at the sound of Stockton's voice.

Slocum got his hand under Rachel's and lifted up and away, twisting to wrest the pistol from her. The Remington discharged again, the heavy ball digging a hole in the ground at their feet.

"Kill them!" shrieked Stockton. "Don't stop, kill them!"

Slocum gathered Rachel up in his arms and carried her away. Bullets began whistling past his ears, making further retreat too dangerous. He fell forward and shielded Rachel from the gunfire until he got inside the burned-out building. Its charred walls provided scant protection, but it did prevent Stockton's gunmen from seeing their targets. If they wanted, however, they could flush Slocum and Rachel out like doves driven out by hunting dogs.

"What got into you?" Slocum demanded. "Stockton would have killed you!"

"I wanted him dead for what he did to me," Rachel said in a voice entirely calm and collected.

Slocum stared at her. Rachel showed no emotion at all.

She might have been telling him she'd gone out for a stroll and visited with friends on a fine Sunday afternoon.

"You aren't hurt, are you?" He didn't think she'd been hit. He saw no blood marring the perfection of her face or body. Still, something struck Slocum as being terribly wrong with the woman.

"Hurt? No. I just wanted to do to him what I did to Pa and Ted and Luke. They raped me, so I killed them. I'm going to kill Ike, too. I am, John. I am."

Slocum stared at her and turned icy inside. Rachel Burnham spoke of killing her father and lover—and who was this Ted? Another lover?—with no emotion.

"Rachel?" he asked.

She smiled, but it was a smile unlike any he'd ever seen. This lacked warmth or the humanity of the woman he'd come to love.

"After I've killed them, I'll kill you, too."

15

Rachel Burnham looked at him as if he were a total stranger. She smiled in a way that gave Slocum chills up and down his spine. He'd never seen such a look on another human being's face—ever. During the War he'd seen his share of men gone crazy with the need to kill. He had seen them dazed and crying and totally adrift in a sea of blood and misery. But he'd never seen a person with the sweet, deadly expression Rachel now showed him.

"It's only right. You raped me. You ought to die for that. And you will."

"Just like Luke and Ted and . . . your pa?"

"Of course, Pa was the first one. When I was nine. Or was it ten?" Rachel frowned, deep in concentration. "I can't seem to remember, but it happened a lot. So I killed him. And Ma, too. She raised such a fuss over me shooting him I had to kill her, too."

"How old were you then?" Slocum's fingers tightened

169

around the butt of his pistol. The woman he loved had turned into something worse than a sidewinder.

"But you know, Pa. You were there. I killed you."

"You were nineteen," Slocum guessed.

"Oh, no," Rachel said, giggling like a little girl hearing a naughty story. "I wasn't more'n sixteen. Billy was only ten."

For the past five years Rachel had gone around with the guilt festering in her brain that she'd killed her father. Slocum didn't want to believe it.

"Why do you keep coming back?" she asked unexpectedly. "You came back when I was seventeen, calling yourself Ted."

"And last year as Luke?"

"Yes! And now you're calling yourself John. But you can't confuse me. You're my pa and you've come back to hurt me again. Only I won't let you!"

With all the fury of a wildcat, Rachel struck out at him. Slocum reacted instinctively. His pistol swung in a short arc. The heavy barrel connected with the side of the woman's head. Rachel crumpled to the ground without uttering another sound. He stood in the sudden silence, outwardly calm but shaking inside. He had no idea at all what to do with the fallen woman.

"Mister, you out there?" came Stockton's voice from inside the barn. "You get the hell away from here and let us be or you'll pay dearly for it, hear?"

"Stockton!" called out Slocum. "The entire town's against you for what you've been doing. No one in Durango will hide you. The New Mexico militia is hot on your trail. You've raped and killed and terrorized enough. Get out now, while you still can."

Stockton's answer came in a deadly rain of bullets. Slocum ducked down, letting the heavy slugs rip away at the

burned-out shell around him. Slocum knew better than to
tangle with Stockton and a livery stable full of his gunmen.
Slocum slipped his arm around Rachel's shoulders, hefted
her to a sitting position, then unceremoniously draped her
over his shoulder. He grunted as he lifted her, then made
as good time as he could back to the *Record* office. Let
Deputy Johnson handle Stockton. Right now, Slocum had
more important matters to attend to.

"Goodness, John, what happened?" cried Mrs. Romney
when he entered the office with Rachel. "Is she hurt?"

He dropped Rachel to the counter. She hung limply, arms
and legs dangling. Mrs. Romney quickly checked the pale
girl, then turned, staring at Slocum curiously. "What's wrong?
I've never seen you look like this."

"Do you know?" he asked.

"What are you talking about?"

"Rachel. She killed her parents. And Luke, and someone
named Ted. Maybe someone called Mase or Mason, too."

"That bullet you took along the top of your head must
still be affecting you. Let me look."

Slocum batted the woman's hand away. "There's nothing
wrong with me. It's her."

"No, John, you're wrong. It's not Rachel."

"What did her pa look like?"

"What? Well, he was tall, about your height and build,
dark hair, and he had a quickness about him."

"Ted? Luke? Both of them looked like her father?"

"Not exactly, but there is a resemblance. You look a bit
like them, but different. Your eyes are green and . . ."

"And we all look enough alike for her to think we're her
father."

"No." Mrs. Romney's voice was small, hardly more than
a squeak.

"What about this Ted? What happened to him?"

"Don't rightly know. He and Rachel went out riding one day. She came back in tears and wouldn't talk about it. I thought they'd had a row and he left her. He wasn't anything but a no-good drifter. Don't know what she saw in him."

"She saw her raping pa in him. And in Luke." Slocum swallowed hard and stared at Rachel's supine body on the counter. "In me, too."

"I knew Ken Burnham," Mrs. Romney said. "He was no prize. I'd be the first to admit that, but you're saying he raped her?"

"Not me claiming it. Her. Rachel said as much."

"It can't be," Mrs. Romney said in a choked voice. But Slocum saw the way her eyes glazed over. It was as if a million pieces fell together for the first time and formed an ugly picture that she couldn't bear. The look of sheer disgust and hatred on the older woman's face directed itself at Rachel.

"Mrs. Romney, Mr. Slocum, they're coming!" came the shout from the door. Billy Burnham stuck his head inside the *Record* office. "Sheriff Watson and his deputy are back. And they been talkin' to Deputy Johnson. I think they're gonna try to smoke out Ike."

The boy stopped and stared at his sister. "What's wrong with Rachel?" he asked. "She ain't been hurt, has she?"

"She . . . she'll be all right, Billy." Mrs. Romney put her arms around the boy and hugged him close. Slocum saw tears running down the editor's cheeks and leaving behind wet, smudged trails that turned black from the ink on her face.

"I'm going to help Sheriff Watson. You look after them. Both of them," Slocum said. The woman nodded, then jerked hard on Billy's arm when the boy tried to spin away.

Slocum checked the load in his pistol as he went. He took the time to duck into a doorway and reload. He wanted to make damned sure that his hammer wouldn't come down on an empty chamber when he needed a shot the most. Satisfied with his load, Slocum raced toward the sheriff's office. He got there just as Sheriff Watson and Sullivan came swinging out the door.

"Get on back to the *Record*, Slocum," Sheriff Watson barked. "We don't need help."

"Just you and him against Stockton and all his men? Or maybe you want to rely on the Committee of Safety for some extra guns?" Slocum pointed at the covered sidewalk across the street where a dozen nervous men gathered. They talked among themselves, whipping up courage with lies and a bottle being passed around.

"Damnation," muttered Sheriff Watson. Louder, he yelled, "All you fellas go on home now. We can take care of this. Git on home!"

"You sure, Sheriff? Just the three of you?"

Sheriff Watson started to correct the man and say two. Then he relented when he saw that Slocum would be worth twice the men gathered in the Committee of Safety. "Get Slocum a rifle," Sheriff Watson called in to his other deputy. Sheriff Johnson poked his head out of the office, a rifle in one hand and a shotgun in the other. He passed the Remington to Slocum.

"Sheriff, I want to come along. You need help. They're mean and they got spooked by the militia. They'll be like cornered rats."

"More like rabid dogs," grumbled Sullivan. "The son of a bitch."

Slocum said nothing. He remembered that Sullivan and Burt Wilkinson had been good friends—and Stockton had turned Wilkinson over to a lynch mob for a paltry reward. He might not like the idea of the deputy going after Stockton for personal vengeance, but Slocum had to admit to himself his own motives weren't lily-white.

The cause of most of his trouble since riding into the San Juan hid out in the stable at the end of the street. And in a way Slocum didn't want to examine too closely, he blamed Stockton for what had happened to Rachel. That was irrational, wrong, but it helped. Blaming Stockton helped.

"Four of us against nine or so of them. Sounds fair to me," Slocum told the sheriff. Watson snorted, then gestured impatiently. The two deputies and Slocum trailed after him to the stable.

Sheriff Watson stood out of the line of fire and yelled to Stockton, "Ike, get your ass out here right now. You're in a world of trouble and if you don't give yourself up, we'll have to come in and drag you out."

A harsh laugh greeted the demand.

To Charlie Johnson he said in a lower voice, "Get on around back. Nobody gets out of there. Nobody, you hear?"

"Yes, sir." Johnson appeared rejuvenated. Slocum nodded. He had seen this before. A man humiliated sometimes snapped back when given the chance. He wouldn't want to be Ike Stockton facing Deputy Johnson now. It wouldn't be much of a match, given Johnson's new determination to do his job.

"Another thing, Charlie. Set fire to the barn. I don't want this lingering till sundown." Sheriff Watson turned and looked over his shoulder to the high mountains in the west. Durango would be plunged into darkness within the hour.

"But, Sheriff, that's Mr. Conroy's property."

"Screw Conroy. I want Stockton!"

Slocum saw the sheriff's point. On all sides Durango lay in ruin. Bullet-ridden walls turned to wormwood, burned-out husks worse than useless, the very streets dug up and made dangerous for man and beast by the fighting all told a sorry tale. One more building burned to the ground wouldn't make a whit of difference.

Johnson went scuttling off. Sheriff Watson pointed and
Sullivan went in the other direction.

"Just you and me, Slocum. Want to make a frontal as-
sault?"

"Let's wait for it to get hot inside," Slocum said. "I
reckon Stockton will be hightailing it out pretty damn soon."

"I hope so." Sheriff Watson fingered his rifle. "When
Sullivan and I were returning to town, we ran across signs
of the militia. Heard tell you already saw them."

"Captain O'Malley and about twenty New Mexico troopers. To the east of here a few days back."

"They had cornered Stockton, but he knew the country
too well for them and got away. Read the signs. Don't think
this Captain O'Malley is going to bypass Durango. When
he gets here, nobody in town's going to let him go un-
challenged."

Slocum saw that the sheriff felt the same way he did
about the Durango Committee of Safety. Vigilante groups
were uncontrollable, no matter if they went out with the
best of intentions.

"Aim for their damn horses," said Sheriff Watson, seeing
the first wispy columns of black smoke coming from behind
the stable.

Gunshots told that Sullivan had thwarted an attempt to
escape to the east. More muffled, deeper ones came from
Johnson's shotgun.

"Here they come!" yelled Sheriff Watson.

The man spun out and levelled his rifle. The doors to
the stable smashed back and four horsemen raced forth.

Slocum had been nervous, expectant, and on edge. No
longer. Old habits returned. A sniper had no nerves; he
killed cold-bloodedly. Slocum raised his Remington,
squeezed off a round, and saw the lead rider throw up his
arms and topple backwards off the horse. A second shot hit
the riderless horse in the shoulder, bringing it down and

forcing the three behind to swerve.

Sheriff Watson's rifle sounded repeatedly, never quite finding a good target. Slocum levered in a new shell, stepped to one side, lifted and fired in a smooth motion. A second man tumbled from the saddle. Cries of anger rose now from Stockton's surviving men.

"Surrender, damn your eyes!" called out Sheriff Watson. His rifle bucked and produced an anguished yelp. A man still on foot in the door of the burning barn clutched his leg and dropped to one side.

Slocum knew they'd been lucky up to this point. All hell broke loose when Stockton's men realized they were not going to be allowed to ride from Durango unscathed.

Pistols scattered lead in all directions. He stood his ground, an emptiness inside demanding filling. For Rachel, for himself, he had to have Stockton's blood.

"There he is," came Sullivan's warning. "Get the son of a bitch. Damn it, get him! Don't let him escape."

Stockton had hung back and let his men draw the early fire, thinking he'd escape easily. Flames all around, a determined sheriff and deputies in front and to the sides, Stockton found himself boxed in. He put his spurs to the horse's flanks in an attempt to break free.

Sullivan's rifle fired four times before jamming. Two of the bullets found Stockton's horse, bringing it down. Stockton rolled forward over the falling horse's head. He hit the ground hard but managed to roll and rob the impact of its full force.

Slocum raised his rifle and saw Stockton's head in a perfect sight picture. The bright bead on the front sight floated just an inch under the man's chin, the V notch centered as good as he'd ever done.

The rifle misfired.

Slocum cursed and threw the Remington aside, going for

his Colt. By the time he had the Colt Navy out, Stockton
had taken cover. Ironically, the man had gone into the same
burned-out building Slocum and Rachel had used earlier.

"Get Sullivan around to the next street," Slocum said.
"Don't let Stockton get away."

Sheriff Watson motioned. Sullivan, the smell of Stockton's blood in his nostrils, already moved in that direction.

Johnson's shotgun blared twice more, a long pause while
he reloaded, then two more explosive shots. What remained
of Stockton's men meekly held up their hands. They saw
too many of their number dead on the Durango street to
continue.

"Charlie, get those owlhoots to the jail pronto. And stay
with them. Don't let the Committee of Safety have them!"

"Yes, sir!" Deputy Johnson herded off the three surviving
members of Stockton's gang. Slocum paid them no attention. The others on the ground stirred sluggishly, severely
wounded, or lay completely unmoving.

"You can't get away from us now, Ike. Don't make us
come for you." Sheriff Watson reloaded his rifle. The set
of his face told Slocum the sheriff wasn't going to let Stockton surrender. Ike Stockton would go into the jail dead or
not at all.

"That smart?" Slocum asked.

"What?"

They locked eyes. Sheriff Watson knew exactly what
Slocum meant.

"I've got duty to do," the man said. "But Ike's gone past
the limits. I used to be his friend. So did Sullivan. So did
most of the people in Durango. He betrayed that trust and
used us."

Slocum knew what the sheriff meant. Laws might or
might not be good, but when a man turns on friends, he's
worse than a criminal. Ike Stockton had become an animal,

a festering sore that had to be removed before peace could return to the San Juan.

"Cover me," Slocum said. Sheriff Watson nodded. Slocum ducked down, dodged past a few wild shots aimed in his general direction by Stockton, then fell belly-down behind a trough not ten feet from the front of the burned-out structure where Stockton took cover.

"Sullivan's coming in behind you!" Slocum shouted. "You're not going to get away, Stockton. Give it up!"

A hail of bullets came ripping through the water trough and forced Slocum to keep his head down. He heard the sound of feet pounding hard and looked up to see Stockton running along the sidewalk, away from him. Stockton fired over his shoulder and sent a cloud of dust into Slocum's face. Sputtering, wiping the dirt from his eyes, Slocum fought to get his vision back.

Slocum's Colt came up. A shot rang out and Stockton went tumbling. Slocum stared at his pistol, then got to his feet. He hadn't fired. Sheriff Watson had winged the running Stockton with a clean shot that took the man high in the thigh.

Sullivan came charging through the ruined building and stumbled out, covered with soot, pistol in hand and ready.

"No!" Sheriff Watson said. His voice carried a snap of command with it. Slocum saw how hard Sullivan fought to keep from pulling the trigger. Stockton lay sprawled on the wood walkway, his pistol flung ten feet away. Ike Stockton clutched his leg. The trouser leg had already soaked with blood. Slocum saw bright red spurting from between Stockton's clenched fingers.

"You hit an artery. He's going to bleed to death unless you do something."

"Sullivan, get Doc Barrett. I don't want Ike dying like that on me. He's gonna stand trial."

The forlorn expression on Stockton's face belied the trouble he had caused throughout San Juan County, in Durango and Silverton, throughout the entire San Juan Basin. Even as Slocum watched, Stockton's face turned whiter.

Slocum dropped down and fastened a tourniquet around the wounded man's upper thigh. This held until the doctor arrived.

Slocum gratefully turned over the responsibility for Stockton to Dr. Barrett.

He knew only part of his problems had been solved. He still had to deal with Rachel Burnham. But how?

Steps heavier than lead, John Slocum went back to the *Record*.

16

"There it is," said Mrs. Romney. "This has to be the biggest headline the *Record* has ever run." She held the still-damp paper at arm's length and stared at it. No victory shone in her eyes.

Slocum knew why—and it had nothing to do with the triumph of scooping all the other papers in the region on the capture of Ike Stockton and many of his men.

"Looks mighty good," Slocum said.

"STOCKTON SHOT, CAPTURED" the headline read. The story went on to detail how Stockton and his henchmen had come to fall into the capable hands of Sheriff Watson.

"Mrs. Romney," came a tired voice from the doorway. They turned to see the hero of the story standing with hat in hands. He had aged a dozen years since Slocum had first seen the sheriff.

"Come in, Sheriff. You look all tuckered out. A cup of coffee will perk you up." She gestured. Billy went off to get the man the coffee. Slocum put his own cup down. He'd barely touched it.

Sheriff Watson glanced at the headlines. "You're going to have to change it a mite."

"What happened?"

"Doc Barrett couldn't stop the bleeding. Said I shot through the *fee*moral artery. He took off the leg with his saw. One of those damned messy things."

"And?" urged Mrs. Romney.

"Ike's dead. Nothing the doc could do worked. Ike died. Hope that doesn't ruin your headline."

"I just print what's news, Sheriff. This will go in as a sidebar. An important one, though."

"There's some more. We let Stockton's men go when Ike died. Didn't figure there'd be any need to hold them with their boss gone."

Slocum asked, "What about the militia? Captain O'Malley is still roaming the countryside looking for Stockton."

"That's the second part of what I wanted to tell you," said the sheriff. "Stockton's men got half a mile back toward Animas City when the militia ambushed them. Killed every last one of them without even asking if they wanted to give up, from the account we got. Josh Sands was riding back and saw it all. We're getting a few of those Committee of Safety men together and going after the militia. Don't care if they wear uniforms or not. They murdered those men. Wired Governor Pitkin to tell him what's been happening."

"That worthless good-for-nothing's not going to support you, Sheriff. Don't do it. Let the militia get back into New Mexico. You'll only make matters worse if you go after them."

"Have to go, Mrs. Romney."

"Please don't." Mrs. Romney took Sheriff Watson's hand in hers and squeezed. "Too many have died. Durango's been shot up good. Don't make it worse. I don't want to see you follow after Ike."

"Kind of you to say that, Mrs. Romney."

Slocum saw that there was more, much more between the two. It made him all the more desolate. Mrs. Romney and Sheriff Watson had one another. He had thought he and Rachel were intended for one another, too. He'd been wrong. Almost dead wrong.

"I got to go, Mrs. Romney. You might be right, but there's the law to consider. This Captain O'Malley should be brought to trial, him and his men having no legal status in Colorado. But I'll take care. This old fox has more cunning than any wet-behind-the-ears militiaman sent by Lew Wallace."

Sheriff Watson left. Slocum saw tears in Mrs. Romney's eyes.

"Chances are good," Slocum said, "that the militia will be back across the border before sunup. They can claim they did their duty. Everyone will be slapping each other on the back and saying they won. Wait and see."

"You might be right, John."

"I am. When you put it on the wire and the *Santa Fe New Mexican* and the *Las Vegas Optic* pick it up, the story'll change. Lew Wallace will claim victory. Those people down in Farmington will claim victory. They all will."

"No one's won," she said heavily.

"There are enough losers in this to keep everyone looking for a victor. They don't understand." Slocum sipped at his coffee without tasting it. "There can be losers with no one winning. That's what's happened."

"Mr. Slocum," spoke up Billy. "You're leaving, aren't you?"

"I'm one of the losers." His voice barely escaped his throat.

"Billy, let me and John talk this over. You go watch over your sister."

"No! I'm no little kid to be pushed around like you always

do. I don't understand what's going on, that's all." He stood
with hands balled at his side.

"Let him stay," Slocum said. "He has to know."

"What went on between you and Sis?" the boy demanded.

"Rachel claimed she killed . . . Luke, and another man
named Ted." He didn't have the heart to tell the boy the
rest. Let him think only good of his father.

"No!"

"Billy, let him talk. Go on, John." Mrs. Romney leaned
back against the counter, arms folded over her breasts. Her
expression was grimmer than Slocum had ever seen it, even
when Stockton was shooting up Durango. She was taking
all this hard.

"I don't rightly understand what caused it, but she's filled
with a powerful lot of hate. Something awful happened to
her and she takes it out on men who look like me."

"No," the boy said.

"Think on it. Didn't Luke look like me? And this Ted?"

"Don't remember him all that well, but yes, you do look
something like him."

"She's like a bomb waiting to go off. Men who look like
me are a lucifer to her fuse. If she gets riled, she kills. Can't
say Rachel is able to control herself. Don't think she can."

"That's terrible," Billy said. "But I don't believe it. I
don't. Sis is wonderful. She . . . she's kind and good, and
she'd never kill anybody. 'Cept a skunk like Ike Stockton.
After what he did to her, *I'd* have tried to kill him, if I
could. He got what he deserved."

"May have," agreed Slocum. "But that doesn't change
Rachel. She's likely to go on wanting to kill tall, dark-
haired men. In this country there's a goodly number of us,
too."

Silence fell in the *Record* office. Slocum finished the
coffee and put the cup down with a loud click on the desk.

"I'm heading on north, as I'd planned. Don't think any-body'd mind if I kept the horse I took from Stockton's men."

"They probably took that swayback nag of yours," Mrs. Romney said. She reached out and caught his sleeve until he stopped and turned. "Do you have to go? There's a place for you here. You do good work, John. And maybe Rachel will get over this. You can help her. You can, John, if anyone can."

He shook his head. "I'm not able to help her. Might even hurt her more. Not even love's strong enough."

Mrs. Romney slowly nodded. Billy Burnham looked con-fused. Slocum didn't blame the boy. He didn't understand what had gone wrong inside Rachel's head and heart, either. He just knew that leaving was the only way to protect her. If he stayed, one day or one night, she'd try to kill him, just as she had her other lovers—and her pa.

Without him stirring up that inner hatred, Rachel might heal up. Slocum didn't think so, but he hoped she could.

"You'll look after her?" he asked Mrs. Romney.

"You know I will." Tears ran freely down Mrs. Romney's cheeks now.

"Billy." Slocum shook the boy's hand. "You look after Rachel, too, you hear?"

The boy nodded.

Slocum walked on cat feet to the rear of the print shop and opened the door. On the cot where he and Rachel had made love for the first time, the woman lay, haloed by silver moonlight coming in through a high window. He didn't understand how she could look so peaceful, even angelic, lying there asleep, and have such deep hatred burning away inside. Without waking her, he picked up the few belongings he'd accumulated and quietly closed the door.

Slocum said nothing to either Billy or Mrs. Romney as he walked out the side door.

He got on his horse, noticing the lumps in his pocket. He reached inside and pulled out the two pecans Crazy Matt had given him.

Not much to show for all this, he thought. He rode out of Durango, going past the cemetery where Matt lay buried, the bright spring moon shining on the simple headstone. He stopped, peered down at the grave, then cracked the pecans. He worked out the meaty centers, ate one, and dropped the other on the old man's grave.

Slocum turned his horse north, toward Ouray. From there he'd go northeast through Poncha Pass and on to Denver. But he wouldn't stop in the city. He'd go north, to Wyoming and Powder River. Maybe even further north.

Even that wouldn't be far enough away for him to forget Rachel Burnham.

JAKE LOGAN

J.D. HARDIN

"THE MOST EXCITING WESTERN WRITER SINCE LOUIS L'AMOUR"
—JAKE LOGAN

___ 872-16869-7	THE SPIRIT AND THE FLESH	$1.95
___ 867-21226-8	BOBBIES, BAUBLES AND BLOOD	$2.25
___ 06572-3	DEATH LODE	$2.25
___ 06380-1	THE FIREBRANDS	$2.25
___ 06410-7	DOWNRIVER TO HELL	$2.25
___ 06001-2	BIBLES, BULLETS AND BRIDES	$2.25
___ 06331-3	BLOODY TIME IN BLACKTOWER	$2.25
___ 06248-1	HANGMAN'S NOOSE	$2.25
___ 06337-2	THE MAN WITH NO FACE	$2.25
___ 06151-5	SASKATCHEWAN RISING	$2.25
___ 06412-3	BOUNTY HUNTER	$2.50
___ 06743-2	QUEENS OVER DEUCES	$2.50
___ 07017-4	LEAD-LINED COFFINS	$2.50
___ 08013-7	THE WYOMING SPECIAL	$2.50
___ 07259-2	THE PECOS DOLLARS	$2.50
___ 07257-6	SAN JUAN SHOOTOUT	$2.50
___ 07379-3	OUTLAW TRAIL	$2.50
___ 07392-0	THE OZARK OUTLAWS	$2.50
___ 07461-7	TOMBSTONE IN DEADWOOD	$2.50
___ 07381-5	HOMESTEADER'S REVENGE	$2.50
___ 07386-6	COLORADO SILVER QUEEN	$2.50
___ 07790-X	THE BUFFALO SOLDIER	$2.50
___ 07785-3	THE GREAT JEWEL ROBBERY	$2.50
___ 07789-6	THE COCHISE COUNTY WAR	$2.50
___ 07974-0	THE COLORADO STING	$2.50
___ 08032-3	HELL'S BELLE	$2.50

Prices may be slightly higher in Canada.

BERKLEY *Available at your local bookstore or return this form to:*
Book Mailing Service
P.O. Box 690, Rockville Centre, NY 11571

Please send me the titles checked above. I enclose _____. Include 75¢ for postage and handling if one book is ordered; 25¢ per book·for two or more not to exceed $1.75. California, Illinois, New York and Tennessee residents please add sales tax.

NAME_____

ADDRESS_____

CITY_____STATE/ZIP_____

(allow six weeks for delivery.)   **161**